To Carol,

My sister-in-Christ,

you have been so
instrumental in my life
with the miracle of
my baby Gabriel. There will
never be enough thank-you's
for your prayers! God
Heard Them!!

In Question

of

Sunsets

James Graham

authorHOUSE®

AuthorHouse™
1663 Liberty Drive, Suite 200
Bloomington, IN 47403
www.authorhouse.com
Phone: 1-800-839-8640

First published by AuthorHouse 3/19/2009

ISBN: 978-1-4389-6573-4 (sc)

Printed in the United States of America
Bloomington, Indiana

This book is printed on acid-free paper.

About this book

My first novel, *Finding Life*, was a work inspired by a series of miscarriages my wife and I endured. I knew we were not alone in our sufferings; many others have shared the same plight. After all, we lost lives that we never held in our arms and never rocked to sleep at night. Other hearts have not been so protected.

After completing the first book, there were no intentions of ever trying to piece together another yarn. I certainly never imagined that *Finding Life* would become a catalyst for a completely different kind of story and, yet, the story would still be a sequel.

A couple of years after the publication of *Finding Life*, at a time when all hope was lost that we would ever see one of those tiny heartbeats survive, it did. On March 31, 2007, we received the gift of a child whom we named Gabriel James Graham. He came at a bittersweet time. For shortly after his delivery, my father began showing signs of advanced Alzheimer's disease. As I watched him quickly fade away, I wrote the following about the two faces of time that seemed to cross me with an uncanny timing.

I am not sure how to feel about time. In one way, it is a great healer. Yet, in another way, it acts like a constant predator, pecking away at our flesh until we lay feeble and demented. God made it, so I should like it – should I not? But, then I must confess that I do not like spiders. I do not like snakes. And, I do not like death. Although, I feel quite certain I will understand death with complete bliss some day. It is just difficult now, as I sit here trapped in my flesh of clay. It is hard for clay to understand anything.

Thinking about it now, I am not sure if there really is such a thing as death. Maybe it is just something we have made up.

As I read that, it sounds silly. Let me attempt to make some sense of it.

I remember receiving an email a few years ago, that told a story (whether it is true or not, I do not know) about Albert Einstein arguing with one of his professors about good and evil. The professor argued that God could not be good because He created evil. He argued that the many evils, such as the death and suffering of children, cancer, heart disease, murder, abuse, starvation and natural disasters were more than enough proof to show that, if there even is a God, He certainly can't be a good God. Einstein asked the professor a couple of seemingly ridiculous questions: Do you believe in cold? Do you believe in darkness? Of course, the professor answered yes to both. If you do not know the story, take a moment to think about those answers and I'll come back to them in a moment (a variation of this story is also used in the early chapters of In Question of Sunsets).

And so, time has once again left me pondering its true self. When my wife and I went through some difficult times trying to achieve the dream of having a child, folks said, with time, our wounds would heal. With time, our losses would dull, become more of a foggy reminiscence that we keep closed up in a dusty trunk of old memories in an upstairs attic. Some even said that with time anything could happen. We may even have the miracle of a child. So, on March 31 of 2007, time became a great friend. Gabriel James was born and time had healed the losses of the past. Time, to me, at that moment, was good.

It was quite sudden that I saw a different side of time. It seemed more of an adversary, something from which I wanted to escape. If time would slow, or even stop for a short time, my father could see what he had been waiting for with such great anticipation. My father loves babies. I have two older sisters and they have blessed him with grandchildren, which he has thoroughly enjoyed. The only thing missing was a grandchild from me.

Just before my child was born, Dad fell ill, which left his Alzheimer's much more advanced. He was confined to a bed, unable to walk and is quickly losing touch with reality. Sometimes he knows who I am, and holds my hand, while other times his eyes only stare at the ceiling, his pupils rolled up toward his head. Most of the time, he is not with me.

"Be careful, he lashes out sometimes," my mother said as I laid Gabriel next to Dad's head.

"Dad loves babies, even dementia can't change that," I responded.

I continued holding the baby next to Dad's head, but he was somewhere else, his eyes in their usual rolled position.

"Dad, here's the baby. Here's your grandson."

Dad did not respond.

I kept Gabriel there and could not help but think about time. There I was, holding a new life that time had slowly grown inside my wife. Time still has a lot of work to do. Baby Gabriel is not in touch with reality. His brain is not able to comprehend its surroundings; it is not mature enough. He cannot take care of himself. He wears diapers that we have to change for him. He can only eat if we feed him. Sometimes we even have to remind him to swallow. Baby Gabriel will not remember lying next to Dad, because time is still developing that ability.

Then I looked at my father, as he laid there lost in some other universe, not aware that a new life, a life that was just beginning, was lying there next to him. For Dad, time is almost finished. Unlike the baby, it does not have much more work to do. Dad is losing touch with reality. His brain is not able to comprehend its surroundings. It has matured too far. It is demented. Dad cannot take care of himself. He wears a diaper that we have to change for him. He can only eat if we feed him. Sometimes we even have to remind him to swallow. Will Dad remember lying next to Baby Gabriel since time has seemingly taken away that ability?

I was disappointed as I stood there, but I kept the baby next to my father's head. It was for a short moment that time took an unexpected empathy. Dad opened his eyes, looked at me and then looked at the baby. He mumbled something and smiled. He then laid his head close to the baby's soft new skin. He turned and kissed Gabriel on the head before leaving us again. Dad slept. Baby slept.

"Jimmy," my mother said as she shook Dad. "Jimmy, do you know who you just saw?"

Dad did not open his eyes as he whispered, "My grandson."

Einstein asked his professor if there was such a thing as cold. The answer is no. Cold is simply the complete absence of heat. When molecules stop moving, they produce no heat. He asked if there is such a thing as darkness. Again, the answer is no. Darkness is simply the absence of light. Is evil the product of God? No, evil is the absence of God.

Is there such a thing as death? I do not believe so. That is where I place my faith. You may do the same. You may also place your faith in something altogether different.

I wrote this shortly before Dad passed away on June 26, 2007. But, with his final words, overheard by my mother, he unknowingly wrote the end to the story you are about to read.

In some ways, I did not create this story. It came to me in a curious series of introductions to people I was able to meet and know for only a short time.

First, there was Chris, a true man of God, whose testimony stayed in my head and eventually inspired me to begin writing this book. I knew him only briefly before his death. However, with the wisdom he left me, it felt like a lifetime.

Then there was Chance (no connection to Chance Gordon in *Finding Life*), an affable young man with a gentle soul. He left this world much too early when he was killed in an early morning car accident while on his way to work. However, it was the story his mother, Rachel, later shared with me, that provided the absolute clarity of how this story would finally play out, and its ultimate purpose.

What would you do if a stranger approached you after the death of a loved one and said he could arrange for you to see that person again? Could it be possible? Could you feel the brush of your deceased as they move by you? Could you feel their embrace, the beat of their heart and the warmth of their breath against your neck, once more? Could you imagine this happening to you? Maybe it already has.

"Faith has to do with things that are not seen, and hope with things that are not in hand."

Saint Thomas Acquinas

In memory of James L. Graham, Sr.

Prologue

It paints crimsons and lavenders throughout the heavens. Its beauty is beyond even the most gifted of brushstrokes. When trying to capture its splendor, even the likes of Michelangelo, Picasso, Rembrandt and the great Claude Monet become nothing more than crayon strapped lads trying to stay within the lines. It mystifies and, still, enlightens. It is the sunset.

Curiously, when there is a sunset in mortal life, it alludes to the end of a journey, an impending death, or the coming of great loss. These were not the intentions of such rare brilliance. Sunsets are cleansing, a new start, and an object of faith. The generations of mankind have watched the sun disappear, conceding a dark cloak, intertwined with a constellation of shimmering bodies that seem to wink back at us; a kind of Morse code from God saying, "Peace my child, it will rise again, tomorrow." This is a rhetorical faith. Indeed, an easy faith. It happened yesterday, last month, last year, and for the last millennium. It will likely take place again tomorrow. But, real faith is an outcome unknown, a time to worry less about the rising sun and more about the un-traveled road ahead.

"The professor," as his chemistry students at the university affectionately called Michael Valentine, never outwardly professed a belief in a sovereign God. The basis of his reasons had a seemingly strong foundation. A few years prior, the exact day hazed beneath a shroud of more pleasant memories, his only son, Fred, and his daughter-in-law, Carrie, were killed on a rainy drive to work. The lone survivor was Angel, the professor's only grandchild. Scars, however, would not escape her. She suffered one of life's cruelest sentences; she would spend the rest of her days in a chair, wheels powered only by a push, or the growing strength in her arms.

This seemed completely illogical to Mike. How on earth, after Fred and Carrie's emotional struggle to receive her and expending so much toward that goal, could young Angel's life be sentenced to this? Surrounded by gifted intellectuals, he knew these things were simply part of an accidental universe. Life, to him, was nothing more than a card game – some drew good hands and others were destined to lose out. "Pure, dumb luck," as he often said.

Nevertheless, even with these seemingly targeted calamities, the professor always used the word "blessed" when he spoke of his lovely wife, Sharon. She was the believer, always fresh and positive, praising God for His gifts. Her faith, in spite of the heartbreaks that sprang from the dark corners of this world, puzzled Michael. She was, in essence, the last wedge that kept the door of complete disbelief from closing.

In the back of his mind, the professor felt confident that Sharon's conversion to faith was nothing more than another human being who wanted desperately to believe there was more to this life than the here and now. She wanted to find hope that she would see her son again and that he was, as so many Christians traditionally believe, "in a better place."

Mike drew this conclusion from the fact that his beloved Sharon began attending church and talking more about God, only after the deaths of Fred and Carrie. Weakness, he was certain, was the catalyst that caused otherwise levelheaded people to believe there was a Creator who was in control and would one day make everything right.

It was several years later, during Angel's senior year in college, that more bad news arrived. The doctors diagnosed Sharon with breast cancer, which had spread to the rib cage and lungs. The oncologist gave her three months to live.

The professor was numb. Although he professed no belief in God, it did not stop him from crying out, "I was only a child! Yet you have cursed me everyday since. How can there be any good in you?"

However, Sharon's faith never wavered. Certainly, she was concerned about Angel, who had already suffered so many losses. Yet, Sharon knew that few things pleased God more than walking in blind faith. So, she prayed as always, asking God to use her situation as a blessing to somebody, whoever His will.

That blessing seemingly arrived one week later. As Sharon rested in bed, two men walked through the opened door. She did not recognize either of them, yet, for some reason they produced no fear in her. They were impeccably dressed, in ironed suits with neatly tucked hankies in their front pockets. They smiled softly and took a seat on the bed, one on each side.

"Who are you," Sharon asked.

"When the time is right, you will know."

Sharon stared blankly as the men placed their hands upon her shoulder and head. Their touch seemed, for lack of a better description, divine. She could not compare it to any other feeling she had felt in her life.

"This disease is not your end. Not now."

Before she could utter another word, the two men stood and walked quickly from the room.

The commotion of screams and cries brought a herd of nurses running to Sharon's room. The professor was right behind them and quickly made his way to the bed.

"Sharon, darling, what's wrong?"

"A miracle is coming. God's sending me a miracle," she exclaimed.

"It's just the medication," said a nurse from the back. "It causes hallucinations."

The professor stared down at his cheerful wife, not sure what to think.

And so, what seemed to be the great miracle Sharon waited for began to unfold. She tried to talk the doctors into repeating the tests, but they resisted.

Even the professor was not sure the tests needed repeating. He knew the cancer was still there and was fearful of how that might affect Sharon's mentality. He wanted nothing to interfere with Sharon's happiness and peace.

After two weeks, it became clear that something was different about Sharon. Her glow returned and she began talking about the future, something she had avoided since learning of how metastasized the cancer had become. Her energy was back and she insisted on walking up and down the hallways, talking about her miracle to anyone who would listen.

The doctors could not explain this sudden turn of events. They ordered a series of blood tests and called Mike in the next morning to discuss the results.

The sun seemed to rise a little earlier that crisp, late October day, cutting through the half-risen blinds, exposing in its rays an assemblage of dust particles floating about. The doctors found Michael sitting on the side of the bed, drinking coffee with his wife for the first time in weeks. Sharon looked radiant.

The doctor smiled briefly and then returned to his serious demeanor.

"They're clean, all of them. Your cancer has, with no definitive reason or understanding, gone into remission."

The professor and Sharon held each other, both afraid to let go. For weeks, they were planning, in silence, for the inevitable. Now, they received the ultimate second chance.

"I don't know how I could have lived without you," the professor whispered in her ear.

From that day forward, the professor and Sharon lived, really lived, each day, each hour, and each minute. They decided to leave the overpopulated town of Wilmington and return to Sharon's hometown of Beaufort, a more peaceful place where they could fully enjoy each other, without the distraction of a busy city. They would leave their careers behind and buy a pleasant little cottage at the west end of Ann Street, just two blocks from the historic waterfront, a place where time had no say.

The people of Beaufort shielded their waterfront from the eyesores of greedy development. There were no towering condos or gleaming new retail stores. Instead, there was an old fashion courtesy, even in the 50's styled pharmacy where you could still pull up a stool, get a vanilla pop, and talk about the weather. Tom, the pharmacist, filled your meds, filled your glass, and took time to talk as he leaned forward, his elbows crossed against the counter.

It was only a couple of days after moving to Beaufort that Sharon found she could no longer finish unpacking boxes with the professor. Her color faded and a loss of her vigor followed. Initially there was a tortuous dread that both she and the professor dared not speak about. But, as the days crawled by, Sharon gradually faded, a hacking cough giving her and the professor all the proof they needed to know that the unwelcome guest had returned. And this time it would not leave without its captive. Despite it all, Sharon continued to pray and felt a welcomed, yet somehow peculiar, peace.

She spent her last few days lying in a dark hospital room, preferring no lights to expose her failing body. It only took a couple of weeks before she whispered goodbye to Angel and, with that same peculiar smile, sent her last words to the professor who had taken a rare break from Sharon's side, "I am at peace, an incredible peace." She then exhaled for the last time.

As Michael wept, his broken body draped around Sharon, the attending physician entered the room, looked at the monitors surrounding Sharon's lifeless body and noted the time on her chart.

Angel sat on the opposite side of the bed, holding her grandmother's hand. After wiping away a rush of tears, she studied Sharon's hand and fingernails. Her nail beds were deep red, contrasting sharply with the pale skin around them. She kissed Sharon's hand, gently placed it back on the bed, and then wheeled out of the room to find the professor and tell him the news.

Chapter 1

The professor's wearied frame hung like a rain drenched T-shirt, laboring to carry the burden of his new life. His white, thinned hair seemed thinner and the intellectual swagger, what little he allowed himself, was gone. He showed all the appearances of a conquered man. A mound of dirt reminded him of his permanent separation from Sharon. A thousand thoughts ran through his mind. He remembered the first time he saw her and the day he held his baby boy, just minutes after Sharon gave birth. He thought back to the day Angel left rehab and arrived to her new home. The professor had built a ramp for her. She cried. He cried. Resilient, like her grandmother, she was determined to walk through that door again one day. She had no doubt that time would come.

The voices around the professor sounded muffled and distant. He was somewhere else, lost in the memories that would become his dearest and yet, most disheartening companion in life. The first days after her death, he lost her spirit, but strangely, he had some comfort knowing her body, her shell, was still there. He could touch her forehead, hold her hand, and even talk to her as if she were only sleeping. But, now he was losing what remained of her. He would never see her again. In a way, he envied her. She was now resting without pain. Even if it were possible, he would not wish for her to become another Lazarus, calling her back to life, only to suffer through another death at some point. No, the professor knew he had the painful encumbrance of not living longer than Sharon, but instead, dying slower.

Angel sat beside the professor, who was now the only person left that prevented her from being an orphan. She couldn't help but think about that. Now that her grandmother (who had essentially become her mother) was gone, she had only one thin shred of family left. She had heard the stories many times about a spouse mourning to death after losing their most loved one. She knew, all too well, that the brain could do that. It was no different than the man she read about who, through a prank by his friends, thought he had eaten a shrimp. He was, unfortunately, deathly allergic to seafood. He would have been better off taking cyanide or arsenic. But, unbeknownst to him, the piece of food was just a small, thin piece of friend chicken breast. His friends watched in dismay as he broke out in hives, complained of stomach pain and began having diarrhea. This all continued until his throat and tongue swelled, causing him to suffocate to death. It was as if he had actually eaten a piece of fried shrimp. After a medical exam, no trace of seafood was found, only chicken. If a mind could do this, certainly it could stop the mourning from, well, mourning.

Angel bowed her head as the pastor said the final prayer. She did not close her eyes, knowing it would only levy up the hurt until she opened them again, allowing a wave of tears to slide down her face. Behind her, she heard the shuffling of feet, which quickly moved past her and to the mountain of dirt that would shortly be used to cover the coffin. It was a man, a fairly young man, no older than forty-five. His curly brown hair was well trained, without a single strand out of place. His face was smooth with freshly shaved cheeks that showcased eyes of piercing, deep green. His expression was alluring and, yet, tranquil. A persistent smile dominated the right side of the stranger's mouth and a faint sparkle made its home in the right eye, as well. Even his impeccably trimmed eyebrows were cared for with the utmost attention. Angel always noticed eyebrows, mostly because the professor's were always wild and untamed. She tried to persuade him to trim them, but he would have nothing to do with that.

"The great chemists always had wild eyebrows," he joked.

The stranger knelt down as if praying with the others, but instead filled a test tube with dirt from the mound.

What is he doing? Angel wondered as she watched from the corner of her eye.

After capping the tube, he quickly made his way through the crowd and stood at Angel's side. As the pastor finished his prayer, the stranger slid the tube into Angel's hand, along with a folded note.

"Give this to the professor," he whispered. "He'll know what it means."

The professor pushed Angel out of the deep grass around the grave. Neither of them said a word. In addition to the dense gloom surrounding her, Angel was also curious as to what the stranger thought he was doing with dirt from a grave. She was especially curious given that the grave was her grandmother's.

The professor, now depleted of any emotions, continued pushing Angel to the waiting car. It wasn't that she needed the help; he just wasn't sure what to do with the empty void that was now his life. So, he pushed.

Angel sat in the car with her head hung low, examining the test tube in her hand. Everything remained awkwardly quiet as they drove back to the cottage. She dreaded getting there, knowing it would seem empty and lifeless with only her and the professor. It might have been at least a little easier had the house seemed like their home. But instead, given the little time that they had actually lived there, it felt strange and uncomfortable. She could only imagine how much lonelier it would be when she went off to graduate school at the end of the summer. There was no question she would have to move on with her life, she just didn't know where. She prayed it would be the University of Chicago, but they had yet to notify her of her acceptance, or not. That was a letter she had hoped to open with her grandmother, being that Sharon had a way of making Angel feel less nervous about receiving such crucial news. After the doctors told her that she would never walk again, Sharon placed her hands over Angel's ears and said sternly, "Yes you will. God makes that decision." Angel believed her grandmother, and still did.

When the car stopped, they both sat quiet, allowing the sun's heat to warm their legs. Angel could feel only the faintness of heat.

"Granddad," Angel broke the silence.

"Yes, dear."

"A man gave me this at the gravesite. He said to give it to you." Angel handed the test tube filled with dirt to him and then the folded letter.

"Who gave this to you?"

"I didn't know him. But he seemed very…" Angel stopped and thought of the right description. "Pleasant," she concluded.

The professor opened the note and read it slowly.

> *Professor,*
> *I know you will try to dismiss this, but I urge you not to. I want to offer you the chance to see your wife again. It will take some work on your part, but be assured this can happen for you.*
> *Take this tube and meet me tomorrow at the west end*

of Front Street. We will meet at sunset. There will be two chairs waiting for us. When you meet me, I want you to tell me what is in the dirt I have given you. Be specific, it is what you do best. And one more thing, just in case you think this is some cruel joke, I have one word that may change your mind. Beverly.

See you at sunset.

Timothy Lee

Chapter 2

The professor walked in circles. He began in the living room, reviewing in his head the name in the letter, Beverly. He had placed that name away, avoided it, for the past forty years. Why now? He never imagined that part of his life would find him again. It had no right. He adored Sharon more than anything on earth. He wanted nothing to hurt her, especially not his past. Beverly, lovely Beverly. There were times he wanted to tell Sharon; for it was the only secret he hid from her. But, he just couldn't imagine that she would understand. He could not bare the chance that she would look at him differently; that she would have been disappointed in his character. What she thought of him meant everything.

The professor walked to the mantle of the fireplace. He stared at a picture of Sharon and himself. "I should have told her initially," he whispered to himself. His eyes watered, torn between the emotions of losing her and the new reminder that he had hidden such a considerable secret for so many years. *Life would have been so different*, he thought. He was thankful it was Sharon who helped write the story of his life. He only wished he could have told her everything. But that was a chance he did not take. Instead, he swept that name under the rug and hoped never to hear it again.

The house began feeling more closed and viscid. The sobering reality of being companionless and the pain of faded memories were not a congenial pair. The professor needed fresh air, so he grabbed the tube of dirt and walked the short distance to the waterfront. It was a warm afternoon, filled with the music of grasshoppers, singing birds and laughter. The professor heard none of these things. Instead, his mind remained preoccupied with the contending emotions of burying his best friend and the audacity of a stranger bringing up things buried long before.

When the professor reached the waterfront, he walked to the west end where he was to meet the stranger the following day. Who was the person behind this? What kind of person would promise the impossible, the one thing that would make the mournful most appreciative and yet, go even further by using blackmail and festering old wounds?

The salty air blew off Taylor's Creek, making the professor's hair join in with the marsh grass as they frolicked back and forth. His round, thin wired glasses collected the salty residue causing him to wipe them clean with his white-collared shirt. Along the marsh was a live oak, its branches shading a bed of oysters and two decaying rocking chairs lying upside down. They had only a few speckles of paint left on their moldering wood. The professor was sure the chairs could tell many stories of the folks that rocked in them over the years.

The professor walked back to the cottage, his head flexed downward, studying the dirt and broken asphalt along the way. He had no interest in the lush green trees, hummingbirds and other noises that presented themselves with summer. When he made it home, he saw an elderly man sitting next door. He had not realized -- mostly because of his scattered emotions -- that his neighbors, whom he had never met, were in town. He quickly began to realize how close together the cottages were along Ann Street. There were barely ten feet separating the houses. He knew sitting on the front porch would mean awkward conversations with whoever was out there.

"Howdy, neighbor," the old man said while tapping the bill of his hat.

"Good afternoon," the professor said in a polite manner. He sat down in one of the porch chairs and looked out across the street.

"So, you're the man they call 'the professor.' I'm Buddy. I hear you moved here from the city."

The professor continued to gaze forward, "If you consider Wilmington a city."

"Oh yeah, it's a city alright. A city compared to this place."

"How long have you lived here?"

"All my life; grew up here, in fact."

"Why haven't I seen you here before?" the professor asked, mostly to make neighborly conversation.

"Just got back from Florida."

"Vacation?"

"Nope. Lady hunting."

"Excuse me?"

"Retirement homes – all over the place. It's like hunting 'coons in a zoo. And I'm a big gamer."

The professor took a moment to study the man more closely. *He has to be in his mid-eighties,* the professor thought.

"You need to watch out for Clover. He lives in the house on the other side of you."

"Why do I need to worry about him?"

"He's a back stabbing gyp."

Gyp? The professor ignored the strange word, pulled the tube from his pocket and began studying it. "What makes you say that about him?"

"He's been trying to steal my lady for years."

"I see," the professor said, still rolling the tube back and forth in his hand.

"Louise is too good for a cheat like him. Wished we could've left him in the everglades. He'd probably try to sweet talk those gators, knowing him. You married?"

"Yes," the professor looked up. "Well, used to be. My wife died recently."

"You two got along?"

"Of course," the professor barked. Embarrassed by his outburst, he collected himself before continuing, "We got along very well."

"Well, in that case I'm sorry you lost her. They say there are only two kinds of widows, or in your case a widow…" The man took his hat off and scratched his head, trying to think of the correct term. "Wi-dow-ee," he said slowly and then smiled to himself that he could think of such difficult words.

The professor looked away from the test tube in his hand and rolled his eyes. "Widower," he said under his breath.

"Yeah, that's what you are, a widowee. Maybe you should call me the professor, too."

The professor sat in silence.

"What was I saying?" Buddy again took his hat off and scratched his smooth head. "Oh yes, widow-ee's. There's two types: the bereaved and the relieved." The old man leaned forward and held up a wood saw. He licked his thumb and index finger before running them down the teeth of the saw. "People shouldn't be acting all pretty to my lady."

The professor looked over at the man, certain he was crazy. He continued sitting in silence.

Buddy focused his eyes, exchanging looks with and without his reading glasses. "Here comes the back stabber right now. Look at him trying to bamboozle my lady."

"Bamboozle?" The professor had to say something about this word.

The old man pulled out a set of binoculars and looked down the street at the couple. "We have our own language down here. You better get used to it."

The professor was not sure what to think about the strange man. Why did he have a saw? "Is she your wife?" he asked.

"Wife," Buddy said in a higher voice. "Why would I want to go and mess up a completely good relationship?"

The professor rocked back in his chair, somewhat nervous about his eccentric neighbor.

"Don't let him fool you. All those two care about is her cooking," said a feeble voice from between the houses. It was an even older man. His body was thin and fragile. Age spots covered his hands, while a thick sweater covered up his arms. "That's all these young people think about these days, I tell you." The old man's bottom lip moved back and forth, covering his upper lip with perfect rhythm. "Those two aren't bamboozling me."

Bamboozle, again? The professor studied the word in syllables, tried breaking it down into Latin, but still could not place a meaning to it.

"My Uncle Frank," Buddy said without taking his eyes away from the binoculars. "He's ninety-eight. I'm eighty-one and he still thinks I'm a kid."

The elderly man continued talking to nobody particular, seemingly more to himself, before crossing his arms and chattering his gums. "Too darn cold out here. I'm tired of you two jabbering anyway." Nobody had said a word.

The professor looked up at his temperature gauge. It was eighty-seven degrees. Frank shuffled his feet toward his house, which was just behind the professor's. "Nice talking to you," the professor said.

"He can't hear you," said Buddy. "Deaf as a door knob."

"Isn't it dead as a door knob?"

"He's ninety-eight, take your pick," Buddy said, more like a blow-off than an answer. He had more important things to concentrate on.

When Clover and Louise got closer to him, Buddy quickly hid his binoculars and sat down in his green metal rocking chair. He began shaving a branch with his pocketknife, acting as though he did not see the two coming.

"Well, good afternoon to you, Louise," Buddy said, pretending he was surprised by her presence.

"And to you, too," she smiled. Clover, a hat covering his frenzied grey hair, looked around the back of Louise so she could not see him. He then stuck his tongue out at Buddy and mocked him with a variety of facial expressions.

Buddy was noticeably angered, but somehow continued smiling through his teeth at Louise.

The professor sat quiet, uncomfortable with the sudden tension in the air.

"And who might this be," Louise asked, her voice sweet with the slightest of a southern drawl.

"I'm Mike Valentine. Pleased to meet you," the professor answered politely.

"You're the professor I've heard about. I'm sorry about your wife."

"Thank you," the professor said, not sure how word spread so quickly about him.

"May I cook you dinner tonight? Think of it as a welcome to the neighborhood gift."

The professor looked over at Buddy who barely lifted the saw and nodded his head no.

"Thanks for the offer, but I can't tonight."

"Just let me know when you're free," Louise answered back.

From behind her, Clover gave the professor an evil eye, making it clear that no one was to have dinner with his woman.

A geriatric love triangle, the professor thought. *That's just what I need.*

Clover gave Louise a kiss on the cheek before walking her to the outline of flowers along her walkway. She smiled and waved at Buddy and the professor. She liked the attention of men, even though they were, at least, fifteen years her senior.

Clover strutted across the street until he got a hitch in his hip. He limped around in a circle until things abated and then headed up the wooden steps leading to his house. He stopped just short of the mat in front of his door. "It was such a lovely time today. I do believe I'll be invited to dinner anytime now. Salisbury steak and red potatoes, I heard her say. Should I save you a nibble, Buddy?"

"Kiss my hammer toe," Buddy shouted back. "She doesn't want a worn out piece of junk like you. You're so old you get winded playing checkers."

"Such a child, you are. Now, if you don't mind, I need to shower and shave before my evening begins."

Clover took a step toward the mat.

"Now you see him," Buddy said, twirling his wood saw around by the handle.

Clover stepped on the mat and abruptly disappeared through a hole hidden under it. The professor could not believe his eyes. Buddy had sawed a hole in the wooden porch and placed the mat over it like a trap.

Clover moaned from somewhere under the porch.

Buddy smiled at the professor. "Now you don't."

Chapter 3

Angel opened the front door and found the professor balancing on one leg, using the other to tap around the mat.

"What are you doing, Grandpa?"

"Don't ask," he said, continuing to examine the front mat.

Angel looked down and then pushed her way through the front door. "Let's go for a walk," she said, tugging at the professor's arm.

The professor looked inside the empty cottage. "That sounds like a good idea."

A warm breeze meandered through the maze of live oaks along Ann Street. Angel closed her eyes and imagined that she was walking through the light gust. She did this often. She learned the technique in her studies of neuropsychology; a program she hoped to soon study further at one of the nation's top graduate schools.

Angel had discovered that a simple thought, vividly imagined, has the ability to change the autonomic functions of the body. She demonstrated this in an experiment by having a series of people imagine biting into a sour lemon and having its juices spray inside their mouths. They then documented if they felt any changes. Everyone had the same result – their mouths began to water. She concluded that a simple thought could cause salivation without an actual food, in this case a lemon, to cause it. And, not only that, she found that the more detailed the thought was, the more response the subject had. Some people concentrated so hard they actually drooled upon themselves. Even after her graduation, Angel continued to perform studies at a local nursing home in Raleigh. She gathered a group of volunteers who had disabilities from previous strokes. Angel led the group through a series of vivid meditations, visualizing themselves using their affected arms and legs again. Amazingly, the entire group began to see improvement.

"Over there," the professor said, startling Angel from her exercise.

"That's a beautiful church. I wonder how old it is."

"Started in 1778," the professor answered, his attention turned upward at the tall, wooden steeple.

"Did you take the historic tour while I was away?" Angel asked.

The professor ignored her question. "A Bishop named Asbury, he was some big name from Europe, came to Beaufort to visit the church in 1785. When he left he said, 'The people are kind, but have little religion'."

"That wasn't nice," Angel commented.

"It's just another church 'leader' thinking they have the right to judge others," the professor said. "He later came back and gave the church a passing grade. He said the Lord had put forth His power and, I forget, something else about the people being good servants and what not."

Angel knew the professor did not forget anything he learned. He was one of the rare people who truly had a photographic memory. His science library contained hundreds of texts. To entertain his guests he would have them pick a random book from his collection and open it to any page they wanted. He would then have them read the first sentence of the page before he interrupted and finished the page verbatim.

"You sound like you really care about this church," Angel said, seeing through his superficial resentment.

The professor waved her off. "It has a place in my heart, but only for its history. Not because it's a church, by any means." The professor led Angel up the handicap ramp, leading from the left side of the stairs. Once he made it to the front door, he read the sign showing it closed at 5:00pm. Even so, he rattled the doorknob and was surprised when the door opened with a creak that left no question as to its age.

"Should we go inside, Grandpa?" Angel asked.

"It's open. I don't see why not."

Once inside the professor ran his hand along the old wooden pews. He stopped halfway down the aisle and looked up at the stain-glassed windows.

"They're glowing," Angel said with astonishment. "It's beautiful, Grandpa."

"Yes it is," he agreed. "Those stained glass windows are irreplaceable. They were put through the fire process twice, instead of the usual once. They were then hand painted, which gives them a peculiar ability to let off a self-perpetuated glow. This happens only at sunset."

"It's amazing," Angel agreed.

"You can also see anchors, nautical devices and pagodas in the designs," a young man's voiced came from somewhere behind the professor and Angel.

"They reflect the history of the early Beaufort port," the professor added while turning around to see who was behind him. "And who are you, young man?"

"I'm Jack. And you?"

"Michael Valentine."

"Michael Valentine," Jack said slowly, almost disparagingly.

The professor sensed Jack's subtle disregard for his name. "Do you not like my name, son?"

"I've heard better." Jack looked down at the floor and gently kicked the carpet. "Nothing personal. It has nothing to do with you."

"Why would I take it personally?"

"You shouldn't."

There was a long moment of awkward silence before Angel turned her wheelchair around to face the young man. "Do you work here, this late?" she asked.

"Sometimes," he answered. "I tend to the old gravesites and sometimes give tours to the visitors. There was a wedding today and I have to clean up before people come to church tomorrow."

"So, you're really working the graveyard shift, aren't you?" the professor half joked. "How did you come across this job?"

"It's not really a job," the young man answered.

"Then what is it?" the professor continued his prodding.

"Community service."

"Community service? Have you been a sinful young man, Jack?"

"Grew up on the wrong side of the tracks," Jack answered, also half jokingly.

His statement perked Angel's attention. She was always, unbeknownst to them, making people into study subjects. "And why do you say that, Jack?" she asked.

Jack returned to his chore of sweeping the main isle. "Because it's true."

"And that makes you do community service?" Angel continued her interview.

"No. Breaking in here and trashing the place got me community service."

"Sounds like you should be scrubbing toilets across the street," the professor jumped in, referring to the county jail across from the church.

Angel lightly hit the professor on the arm before turning her attention back to Jack. "Did you go to jail?"

"Would have, but the church dropped the charges. They instead offered to have me tend to the place."

"They really trust you to do that?" the professor again interrupted Angel's questioning.

"I made a mistake; hung out with a bad crowd, I guess. It's all I know. Pastor Eric is a good man. He could have easily let me rot with the other convicts."

"And what did the pastor say when he first talked to you," Angel continued.

"He said he wanted to change my name to some guy named Reuben in the Bible."

"Why did he want to do that?"

"He said I was like water. Water doesn't have a hard shape unless it's frozen. And, even then it takes the shape of its container."

"So, you're easily influenced," Angel answered. "That's what Jacob said about his son, Reuben."

"It took me weeks to figure that out," Jack said, impressed at how easily Angel put the comparisons together. "Pastor Eric made me a deal. He said I had a week to figure out why he would name me after Jacob's son. I guess he really made it easy for me, the answer was at least in Genesis." Jack looked at the professor. "I'm not a fast reader, especially with the Bible. It's kind of Greek to me."

The professor looked unimpressed by the story and with the boy, for that matter. "Its translations were from Greek, if that makes you feel better."

Jack wasn't sure what to make of the professor's comment. "So, enough about me, how do you know so much about this old church?"

The professor continued studying the windows. "Got married here a long time ago," he finally answered.

"In 1778?" Jack said with a smile.

The professor briefly looked back at the boy and then pretended to ignore his joke.

"You have a nice smile for a boy from the wrong side of the tracks," Angel remarked, before realizing what the professor said. "You married Grandma in here?"

"Yes," he answered, "and not in 1778. It's time to go, Angel. Nice meeting you Jake."

"Jack," Angel corrected him while smiling at the young man. "And I'm Angel."

Jack smiled again, this time with a thankful glance at Angel. "Angel – now that's a name I like."

Chapter 4

The professor paced the house for most of the day. *Who is this Timothy Lee? And what did he really want?*

When the sun began its decent, the professor grabbed the test tube of dirt and stormed from the house. The door slammed behind him, waking Buddy from his afternoon nap on the porch.

"Professor, you look madder than a mule chewing on bumblebees," he said in between yawns.

"I don't have time for your games," the professor muttered.

Buddy perked up. "Don't have time for my games? My games?"

"You heard me." The professor paused to let a car go by.

Buddy picked up his wood saw and ran his fingers down the blade.

Without looking back, the professor said, "Don't think about it. I'll wrap that saw around your neck."

A confused look came across Buddy's face. "That's not very neighborly." He looked down at the saw, shrugged his shoulders, and placed it back under his rocker. "Somebody's acting crazier than a sprayed roach," he said under his breath. "And it's not me."

When the professor arrived at the end of Front Street, he noticed that the two worn chairs were gone from the marsh grass. In their place were two shiny, white rocking chairs, just a little ways up the bank, cuddled under the shade of a live oak tree. He looked around to find the old, paint-chipped chairs he had come across the day before, but they were nowhere in sight.

The professor continued looking around, but saw no one. "He's not even going to show up," he said with a snarl. He then sat down and put his head in his hands, fighting back tears of frustration and anger. He felt like screaming at the world. If only he could hurt it, but no, he could only be a fly, a pest, upon the king's stately horse. "I hate this world," the professor muttered.

"Ah, but the world does not hate you, my friend."

The professor lifted his head from his hands and looked into the calm of a stranger. Just as Angel had described, he was a fairly young man, no older than forty-five. His curly brown hair was well trained -- not a single strand out of place. His face was smooth with freshly shaved cheeks that show-cased eyes of piercing, deep green. His expression was alluring and, yet, tranquil. A persistent smile dominated the right side of the stranger's mouth and a faint sparkle made its home in the right eye, as well. Even his impeccably trimmed eyebrows were cared for with the utmost attention.

"Who are you," the professor asked, pausing briefly between each word.

"I am who I said I was," the stranger answered, again with a pleasant smile. "I'm glad you made it, professor."

The professor's growing anger traveled from his rigid neck up to his blood shot eyes. His blood boiled. "I came here to tell you to stay out of my life and leave my family alone."

"Professor, I assure you. I can help you get through your grief and allow you to see your wife again."

The professor exploded out of his chair and grabbed the man by his shoulders. The stranger made no attempt to resist. The professor gripped harder, but the stranger continued smiling, showing no sign of resistance. Not accustomed to, and not tolerating aggression, the professor loosened his hand from the man's torso.

"My wife is dead. Why will you not allow her to rest in peace? Why will you not allow my family our time to mourn? Are you that sinister?"

"Professor," the stranger began with a slight European accent in his speech, "I am not here to further scar the heartbroken. I am here to help you."

"Help me? You bring back my painful past and say you're here to help me?"

"A miracle for you."

"There are no miracles," the professor shot back, his voice cracking with frustration.

"But there are," the stranger persisted. "There are miracles all around you. You just need to know what to look for."

The professor shook his head in disgust and abruptly turned around and began walking away. "You've wasted enough of my time."

"She was special, that Beverly. Wasn't she?"

The professor looked up to the sky and stopped walking. "How do you know about her?"

"I have my ways." The stranger's smile never changed. Even with the professor's hostility, he remained very pleasant.

The professor turned around and walked toward the man.

"I believe this may be of interest to you," the stranger said, fanning through the pages of a worn book as if it were a deck of cards.

The professor saw a book in the man's hand. Its leather was cracked and faded, obviously worn from years of use. It was Sharon's Bible. "How did you get that?"

"From your wife, of course."

"That doesn't belong to you." The professor snatched the book out of the man's hand.

"You are correct, professor. She wanted me to give it to you."

"How do you know my wife? And how do you know about," the professor cleared his throat. "How do you know about Beverly?"

"Professor," the man's smile became slightly more defined, "it really is a small world."

"Why are you doing this? Who are you?"

"My name is Timothy Lee and I'm a fisherman."

"A fisherman?" The professor's head began to spin. *Who is this person?* "What kind of fisherman?"

"A fisherman," the stranger said again. "I fish all up and down this waterfront."

"Tell me how you know...all of this."

"In time," the stranger answered. "For now we have work to do. Did you bring the dirt I gave you?"

The professor said nothing as he pulled the tube out of his pocket.

"Very well, then. Let's get started. Your wife looks forward to seeing you."

"She's gone," the professor said, this time with a hint of weariness in his voice.

"No, professor. She's with God. And God still talks to his children. You just need to know how to listen."

"There is no God," the professor said. "No 'good god' could allow a woman as good and faithful as my wife to die like she did. It doesn't make sense and," the professor looked in the eyes of the stranger, "neither do you. I don't know who you are and I don't care. This charade is over."

"I tell you the truth, professor. I'm here to help you see your wife again. She needs you to know that she's okay."

The professor turned around and glared at Timothy Lee. "I'm calling the police," he said, before walking back towards his cottage.

"Professor, you were gone when she passed. You didn't get a chance…"

"Everybody knew I was gone when she died. Don't try to look like some modern day prophet. You're just another gypsy; a sick one at that." The professor continued walking.

Timothy Lee stood and spoke louder so the professor, who was now a good distance away, could hear him. "There was a young man who had a difficult decision to make. The decision, he knew, would affect not only his life, but more so, the life of two others. After he followed his heart, he began hating himself. Even today, he does not feel worthy of anyone's love. Yet, he was given the finest love any man could covet."

The professor stopped, but still did not turn around.

The stranger walked closer to him. "It was a dark time, I know."

The professor closed his eyes. He felt the world begin to spin.

"Dark times indeed, my friend. I know dark times, myself. When I was a child, my family and I traveled to a place called Humpback Mountain and visited its Linville Caverns. The caverns were tunnels that traveled far beneath the mountains. I was young and curious and, at the time, had no fears. I had never been afraid before. I knew that no matter what, my mother and father would protect me. So, I wandered away from the group and began exploring the caverns. Before anyone noticed, I was deep in the mountain, turned around and lost in its maze and unable to be heard. It was so dark I could not see my hand, even when it was almost touching my eyes. Not even a silhouette could I see. It was called ground zero; it was complete darkness. Not even a trifle of light was present. It was so dark that the trout, swimming in cold streams through the tunnels, were blind. In fact, if I had stayed in that darkness long enough, my eyes would have stopped working and, like the fish, I would have gone blind."

The professor opened his eyes and decided to finish listening to the stranger's story.

"That was the first time in my life that I was really scared. And, to this day, it remains the most frightened moment of my life. When they found me and I saw the flicker of light from a candle pierce the thick darkness, a wave of emotions rushed over me. The feeling was euphoric. I still get chillbumps just thinking about it. That small flicker of light led me back to the entrance of the cavern. But, it was only after I stepped into the full light of day that I broke down. I cried, professor. I never wanted to be away from that light again."

The professor listened.

Timothy Lee continued, "As evil as things seem and as lost as these things make us feel, there will come a light, a candle, if you will. However, many of us will not recognize the candle. Its light will not be as obvious as it was in those dark tunnels of the caverns. You're thinking that your candle has burned out, that it was buried and stifled."

The professor pressed his palms across his forehead. He developed the nervous habit during his years in chemical research.

"Professor, your candle is still with you and it wants to show you that its glow is only a tiny part of a much greater light. Don't blow it out because you think she's gone. Remember, things are not always what they seem to be."

Timothy Lee sat back in his rocker and grabbed the tube of dirt the professor left in the other chair. He opened the top and allowed some of its contents to run through his fingers. A quiet breeze found its way to the filtering dirt and twirled it through the air until it thinned into a mist and subtly disappeared.

"Dust," the stranger whispered. He then stood and began walking toward the professor. Sheets of dirt continued whisking away in the breeze. "Professor, may I ask you a question?"

The professor remained standing in silence.

"Professor," the stranger began as he sifted through the dirt, "what's the most abundant chemical in the body?"

The professor was unstirred and made no reply.

"Oxygen," the stranger answered for him. "Interesting," he continued. "And this dirt I'm holding, what's the most abundant chemical in it?"

The professor remembered the dirt and from where it came. He still did not turn around to look at the stranger. He broke the silence with a quiet voice that grew stronger with each word. "You spend all this time telling me that I'm going to see my wife again and now you're telling me she's becoming dirt?" The professor shook his head slowly. "Now I get it. Dust to dust. My wife's body is turning back into the dust of the earth and when I want to see her and talk to her, all I have to do is go back to the grave and talk to the dirt." The professor slid his shoe across the dirt. "Such wisdom. How can I ever thank you enough?"

"Interesting, but no," said Timothy Lee. "Please don't take this the wrong way, professor. I'm just a little curious. I don't get the opportunity to talk with a real scientist everyday."

The professor placed his hand over his eyes, but continued listening to what this mystery man would say next.

"So, professor, I was just reading about this study done at one of NASA's research facilities in California. Some scientists identified all the chemicals in the human body and then compared these with ones found in the dirt." Timothy Lee chuckled before going further. "It's a little humorous, you know, that anyone would spend time and taxpayer's money comparing the makeup of dirt to that of the human body." Timothy Lee laughed louder as he said, "Dust of the earth and all that nonsense. Either way, they're both just a bunch of lifeless chemicals. Nevertheless, it is interesting. The scientists discovered that all the chemicals in the body are found, strangely enough, in the earth's crust. Crazy, I know."

Timothy Lee poured the dirt from the tube on the ground and began smoothing it down with his hand. He then began writing in the dirt with his finger. He looked up at the professor, whose back was still facing him, and smiled. "What do you say we meet back here tomorrow, sunset? Maybe then you can tell me where your faith is."

The professor continued standing with his head down, replaying the conversation in his mind. He processed and studied all the words, trying to find a clue that would solve this mystery. Then he remembered the stranger commenting that the chemicals in dirt and the body were '*lifeless*'. The professor found this curious. The man was no scientist. He was a fisherman. The professor himself had never thought about the fact that his *living* body was made up of *lifeless* chemicals. This was strange to him. It was a scientific contradiction: Life from the lifeless.

The professor turned to inquire why a simple fisherman would find interest in such trivia, but when he did, he saw one of the rocking chairs slowly come to a stop. The man was a hundred yards away, walking back to wherever it was he came from.

The professor walked to the chair, stopped it from rocking, and watched the stranger disappear behind the Maritime Museum. *He got out of here in a hurry,* the professor thought to himself. When he looked down, he saw letters traced in a fresh circle of dirt. The professor focused his eyes and then knelt down to get a closer look at the words. "Genesis 2:7," he whispered.

Chapter 5

Angel grew tired of waiting on the professor. It had become a ritual each afternoon for them to take a stroll along Ann Street. This time she would go alone. As she made her way down the ramp she was somewhat surprised to see Buddy sitting on Clover's porch drinking a soda and having a peaceful conversation.

"More?" Clover asked politely as he filled Buddy's half-empty glass. The ice hissed and crackled under the fresh carbonation.

"Ahhhh," said Buddy. "There's nothing like a strong cola on a hot day." The faded, yellow tint of the glass helped conceal Clover's mischief with the beverage.

Angel paused to make sure she was seeing correctly. When she did, she noticed that Buddy's lips and teeth were green. With each sip, his face and cheeks also began turning green.

Buddy leaned forward and looked Clover in the eyes. "I've got to say, old friend, I'm really humbled that, with me and Louise, you know, being an item tonight, that you are man enough to brush it aside and still be civil about things."

Clover smiled and lifted his glass for a toast. "To maturity," he said as the glasses clanged together. Buddy smiled back, the green color bleeding farther down his chin and neck.

"You know, since we're being civil and all, I have to pay you a compliment," Clover began. "Green is a nice color on you." He looked over at Angel and winked as he mouthed, "Food coloring."

Buddy looked down at his flowery Hawaiian shirt. He then looked back at Clover with noticeably more confidence. "Thank you, friend." He looked back again at the green leaves on his shirt. This time he noticed one of the red flowers had a drop of green color on it. Buddy's smile faded as he used his fingernail in an effort to scrape it off. The green only spread farther. He then licked his finger and again tried to wipe the stain off. This, as before, only made the green spread more. Buddy pondered for a moment and then pretended to pull two guns out of a holster, pointing them at Clover. "It's a good thing I look handsome in green." He then moistened his thumb and ran it across his right eyebrow. "Tell me how fine I'm looking again."

Clover feigned agreement. "You're looking finer than a frog hair split four ways!"

The compliment made Buddy's face light up. "Now, that's fine." He then lifted his shirt and used his thumbs to stretch his pants away from his stomach. "Expandable waistline," he said with a smile. "Elastic on the sides allows your belly to swell with food and you don't even have to loosen your belt." He allowed the elastic bands to snap off his thumbs. "Whoever thought of this was a genius."

Clover smiled. "Almost as good as your glow-in-the-dark sunglasses idea. God only knows how many millions of people wear sunglasses in the dark."

Buddy pursed his lips, contemplating Clover's words. "That reminds me, I need to call that patent lawyer back before somebody steals my idea."

Angel journeyed down Ann Street, taking moments along the way to embrace the summer breezes. Each day at 3:00, she went through a rigorous workout in an effort to strengthen her legs. And, although each day her legs were still not able to hold her once she lets go of her support, she never ceased trying. Staying positive was her passion. So, as she rolled down the street, she repeated to herself, "My legs are growing stronger each day. My legs are growing stronger each day. I have enough strength to begin walking. I have enough strength to begin walking." She called the exercise 'positive affirmations'. She found in her studies that when the brain concentrated on a clear image with words spoken aloud, it would lead in that direction and, with time, make the image a reality. Angel theorized that there were few limitations of a properly exercised brain; the only real limitation was the heart.

Taking a moment to rest her arms, Angel stopped at the corner of Ann and Craven Streets. This was the usual place where she and the professor would stop and, in silence, stare at the Ann Street Church. He thought about his wedding day so many years before, and the dark secret he almost told Sharon that day. Angel thought about Jack.

Angel powered her way up the ramp and quietly opened the door. The church was nearly dark with only a few rays finding strength to pierce the stained glass. At the front of the church, in the pew just behind the grand piano, sat a boy with his head buried in his hands.

"What are you thinking about?"

Jack jumped. "You scared me," he said, noticeably embarrassed.

"Right now, just then. What were you thinking about?"

Jack placed his head back in his hands and then looked back at Angel. "Not a lot goes on up here," he said while pointing to his head.

"Really," Angel continued. "What were you thinking?"

"I was thinking that I have so much work to do and I don't know where to start." Jack tried to seem more chipper as he stood and grabbed his broom.

As the sunset fostered the last few glimmers from the stained glass, Angel looked more closely at the young man. His hair was dirty blonde and looked as if the wind tended to it each morning. Strands of it fell across his eyes, compelling him to toss his head to the side in an effort to see more clearly.

"You're not going to tell me?" Angel asked with a sigh.

"There's not much to tell. But, since we're asking all these questions, how'd you get paralyzed?"

"I'm not," Angel insisted while wriggling her toes. "Paralyzed people can't move their toes."

Jack looked confused. "So, why are you in a wheelchair?"

"It's temporary…until I train my legs to walk again."

"Well, what happened to you legs then?"

Angel stopped and gave a playful smile. "Who's asking the questions here?"

Jack smiled and then tossed a strand of hair from his eyes. "You started it."

"Well, since you're being such a gentleman, I'll tell you. I was in an accident that damaged part of my spinal cord. But, by exercising my legs and having a positive mental attitude, I may walk again."

Jack listened intently. He thought for a moment and then responded: "How long has it been?"

Angel's mood became guarded and defensive. "That's not important. What's important is that I will make it happen." Angel turned her chair around and began rolling toward the exit.

"Wait, Angel. Please," Jack pleaded. "I'm sorry. Whatever I said, I'm sorry."

Angel stopped her wheelchair and took in a deep breath, "No, I'm sorry. I don't like to see that doubt people get in their eyes when they hear me say I will walk again, only to find out I've been stuck here for years."

Jack became self-conscious about the expression on his face and the look in his eyes.

"And then they do that," Angel turned around and said.

"Do what?" Jack acted innocent of any other thoughts.

"They smile and tell me how certain they are that I will do it, even though they don't believe it. I'd rather somebody tell me the truth. Tell me I can't do it. That gives me more motivation than someone feeling pity for me."

Angel and Jack said nothing for a moment; there was just an awkward stare. The old church sat still, as if coercing the two within to break its silence.

"You," Jack said.

Angel looked confused. "Me?"

"You," Jack repeated. "You asked me earlier what I was thinking about. It was you."

Chapter 6

The professor sat on his front porch drinking a glass of sweet tea, compliments from Louise, of course. She "just happened by" earlier, wearing a purple dress and a large, red hat. She was the self-appointed "Honey Bee" of the Beaufort Red Hat Society. As Honey Bee, she felt it was her duty to ensure that every unmarried man, or at least those that had something of use to her, were treated to the occasional home-cooked meal and a never-ending supply of sweet tea. Her favorite catches were carpenters, car repairmen, heating and air conditioner repairmen, and the occasional jackpot – a do-it-all handyman with a variety of talents from locksmithing to foot rubs.

The professor, however, had not thought twice about Louise's neighborly ways. His mind was churning, trying to figure out how Timothy Lee knew so much about his past. Part of him looked forward to meeting with the stranger again. There was not much the professor's scientific mind could not figure out. This, he assured himself, would not go uncovered. But, deep, deep inside, there was a part of him that wanted to believe that he could see his Sharon again.

Buddy and Clover walked out of their front doors at the same time. This was not unexpected, as the professor noticed their routines were the same each day. The only real difference was which one would get the invitation for dinner with Louise.

Buddy looked over at the professor. He gave a half-friendly nod before glancing over at Clover. When the two men made eye contact, both turned their backs to the other and let out indecorous grunts.

The professor smiled to himself. He actually enjoyed the entertainment of his eccentric neighbors. *Listening to these two fools is the only time I have a reprieve from Sharon,* he thought to himself. It was then that he felt a strange presence just over his right shoulder. The professor turned around and, when he did, was startled by the figure standing just inches behind him. His glass of tea sloshed back and forth until a drop spilled out onto his pants.

"Uncle Frank has a habit of sneaking up on people," said Buddy.

The professor, somewhat embarrassed, looked at the mildly startled old man. "I didn't know you were standing there. Are you okay?"

"Not to worry, nothing but a stone in his chest. Old man's going to outlive all of us."

Uncle Frank returned to his usual posture without saying a word. He remained on the professor's porch, just inches behind the rocking chair.

The professor tried to figure out how the old man got up on the porch so quietly. Even though it was only two or three feet high, it was still quite an accomplishment for a ninety-four year old.

Angel rolled up the sidewalk with a pile of books tied to the back of her wheelchair. There was an awkward greeting between her and the professor. She knew the question would come.

"You were out late last night, weren't you?"

Angel rolled her eyes when she reached the top of the porch.

"Hey, sweetie," Clover said to Angel.

Before she could reply, Buddy interrupted, "Hey, honey."

"Are you going to give me any idea where you were all afternoon and half the night?" the professor cut in.

"You need to get use to me not being your little granddaughter anymore. It's called the 'law of acceptance'."

"Well, the 'law of Grandpa' says you need to let me know where you're going after dark."

Angel knew she did not need to add any more stress for the professor to deal with. Stress fatigued the front part of the brain, the pre-fontal cortex, making the brain age faster.

"I was talking with Jack. He's really a nice guy, just needs a little neuropsychology to get him going. He's a stimulating case."

"Who is Jack?"

"From the church."

"Convict," Buddy said, his back still facing away from Clover.

"That Dimmer kid is slicker than snot on a glass doorknob," Clover agreed.

"I hear his daddy died in the pen," said Buddy.

"His momma was all caught up in drugs. She died of an overdose. His grandmother raised him. They say she was a good woman. When she died he was done," Clover added.

"He can't help where he comes from. What matters is where he's going. And he can go anywhere he wants," Angel corrected the men.

"Look's to me that he wants to go to prison," Buddy said with a chuckle.

"That's where you go when you trash a church," Clover again followed up.

The professor looked back and forth at Buddy and Clover before settling his eyes on Angel. "I don't like you keeping such company."

Angel rolled her eyes. "He's an interesting study, that's all. It's probably more important that we evaluate the company you're keeping these days. Tell me about the man you met, the one who sent the note."

The professor stared blankly at Angel before turning his attention to Buddy and Clover. "Do you guys know a Timothy Lee? He's a fisherman that hangs around Front Street."

Buddy stood abruptly and looked over at Clover, who also sat up in his seat. Both of the old men's blood turned cold. Buddy's mouth quivered nervously, unable to find any words.

"Keep that man away from your family," Clover finally said.

After a few attempts to do so, Buddy was finally able to whisper: "Please don't bring that man back around here."

Chapter 7

The professor sat alone in his recliner. His head pounded as he tried to make sense of the situation. Sure, the stranger was different....but, assault and battery? Even worse, on a child? Ten years before, as Clover and Buddy told the story, he shook a neighborhood child so badly that she nearly died from head trauma. The child, as they told it, picked a flower from Timothy Lee's yard. It was enough to make him lose his senses and become enraged with her. The trial gained significant media attention as Timothy Lee's defense team claimed their client, who already had a long list of legal problems, had stopped taking his medications for schizophrenia because he could no longer afford them and refused to ask for help.

The case, as expected, was heated. The entire community was in an uproar. Everybody knew Timothy Lee was a time bomb waiting to go off, but it was too late. A child was nearly killed.

The state's medical team verified that Timothy Lee had, indeed, stopped taking his medications. Expert medical witnesses, on both the defense and plaintiff sides, corroborated that the defendant was not of sound mind when the assault occurred. Experts from both sides also agreed that Timothy Lee was, at the very least, a dangerous and unpredictable man.

It was therefore decided that he be treated in a psychiatric ward and then be reevaluated to determine if he continued to be a perpetual threat to society.

There wasn't much heard from Timothy Lee after that day. Rumors began, as is expected in a small town. Some said he was treated with electric shock therapy and then moved to Utah where he began a family. Others gave different stories. It was said Timothy Lee did indeed undergo shock therapy, but it only made him worse. It was also said that he harmed a nurse and was sent to a high-risk psyche ward in Tennessee. But, the most unnerving rumor was that Timothy Lee was being released to society after a long track record of good behavior. This rumor, as it would turn out, was no rumor at all. Timothy Lee moved back to Carteret County after being absent for ten years. He began working as a fisherman for a local market on Front Street.

The professor chewed on his fingernail as he watched the sun begin its slow descent. He was afraid for Angel. He was afraid for himself and everyone around him. What he kept questioning was, why? Why did Timothy Lee pick him? And, even more mysterious, how did he know things no one, besides the professor himself, should know? He decided he must do something. He thumbed through the phonebook and dialed the number to the local police.

"Yes, this is Michael Valentine. I…," he was not sure how to say it. "I believe…or, I think that I am being stalked by…"

"Mr. Valentine, are you still there?" said the voice of the other end of the line.

"Yes, I…I'm sorry. It's a false alarm."

"Should I send someone to your house, sir?"

"Not necessary," the professor answered. He then hung up the phone and ran his fingers through his hair. He looked at the clock on his wall. "If I don't go to him, he may come to me."

Chapter 8

The professor moved quickly to Front Street and, unlike the time before, found the stranger already waiting for him. He was sitting in the rocking chair reading a paper. The professor walked carefully in front of Timothy Lee and sat in the chair next to him.

"Good afternoon, professor."

The professor had no intention to worsen the situation. He knew that, assuming this individual had mental issues, it was in his best interest not to anger him. Therefore, he decided to go along with whatever the stranger wanted and, with any luck, walk away with his family's safety.

The two men sat in awkward silence for what seemed an eternity. The professor finally spoke. "Reading something interesting?"

Timothy Lee didn't lift his head as he answered, "Actually, I am."

The professor waited for a reply, but grew more nervous as the seconds passed. *Does he know I called the police?* "Feel like sharing?"

Timothy Lee continued reading in silence. After a few minutes, he scribbled something on the folded paper and placed it on the ground.

"Do you ever collect seashells, professor?"

"It's just been a while since I have. When I was a child, I'm sure." The question caught the professor off guard. He expected something different, something more interrogating.

"As a child, you say? Yes, we do a lot of things as children that we don't do as adults. That's really too bad. Would you not agree, professor?"

The professor was not sure how to answer the question, if it was, indeed, a question at all.

"Yes, yes, my, my," the stranger repeated to himself. "If only we could keep our innocence and faith like we had as children." Timothy Lee continued nodding his head. His calm, peaceful disposition never changed. "Yes, children are great, indeed."

The professor could only muster a nod.

"Do you know where I like to find sea shells?" Timothy Lee asked.

"The seashore?" the professor answered, not meaning to be sarcastic.

"That would be the obvious answer, wouldn't it, professor? I'm glad to see you loosen up a little. Yesterday you were quite angry with me and today you act like you're walking on pins and needles."

The professor, of course, only gave a nervous smile.

"So, I enjoy finding seashells on mountain tops. It's interesting finding these so far away from the sounds and oceans."

The professor, after a moment, put the words together. "On top of mountains? Seashells?"

41

The stranger gave a dauntless smile. "Yes, on top of mountains. Did you know that every mountain range in the world has seashells on them? Kind of strange, wouldn't you say, professor?"

"How do…," the professor began to ask before being interrupted.

"Let's meet here tomorrow, sunset. Your wife is waiting patiently. And, I'm still looking forward to hearing where your faith is." Timothy Lee rose from his rocker and walked back toward town. The professor watched until he disappeared behind the pharmacy and then sat back and exhaled. A police car rode slowly toward where the professor was sitting. The officer gave a friendly wave and kept driving.

The professor started to leave when he noticed the rolled up paper Timothy Lee left behind. It was an edition of *The Washington Times*, dated November 18, 1997. The professor read the date and examined the paper from each end. It was strange, he thought, that a paper this old looked as if it were just off the press. He then noticed the title of an article was circled: "CIA Spy Photos Sharpen Focus on Ararat Anomaly."

The professor, still perplexed by the oddity of a person having such an old paper, continued reading slowly to himself. He read about how another professor, Porcher L. Taylor III, from the University of Richmond, fought the CIA for four long years to have pictures released to the public of a strange object on top of Turkey's Mount Ararat. The ice and snow covered peak of the mountain measured at 17,000 feet high. There were a large number of pictures taken by a U-2 spy plane at the end of a 3,000-mile mission from the Soviet Union to Turkey. Mr. Taylor, using the Freedom of Information Act, was able to get those photos released to the public, but not a series of clearer, high-resolution pictures taken during another spy mission.

The professor sat back in the rocking chair, slid his glasses to the tip of his nose, and continued reading the paper. A top CIA official by the name of George Carver stated during a gathering, "there were clear indications that there was something up on Mount Ararat which was rather strange."

Another top ranking official, who decided to keep his name anonymous, told of seeing pictures from KH-9 and KH-11 spy satellites that showed, what appeared to be, wooden beams like those found on a boat. He said, "They sort of curved over and formed up what would have been the bow of something or other poking out of the ice."

In nineteen ninety-one, five archaeologists attempted to hike up the mountain to study the "Ararat Anomaly." Tragically, Kurdish rebels kidnapped the group. This, along with the permanent ice and snow covered peaks, made further exploration difficult.

"How does a boat end up on top of a mountain?" the professor asked himself. He looked down and saw a halved clamshell under the chair Timothy Lee had sat in just minutes before. It was then that the professor remembered being a child and climbing to the top of Grandfather Mountain with his best friend's family. He recalled collecting something that confused him. He and his friend were collecting…something. His brain continued searching. It was something strange. He was very young. He remembered the parents saying it was strange. He thought harder. He opened his eyes. "We found clam shells."

The professor looked back at the paper. He noticed a scribble at the bottom of the page. He focused his eyes and pulled the paper closer. Then he read it: Genesis 7:17-20 and 8:4.

Chapter 9

The professor found himself consumed in Buddy and Clover's conversation. He was accustomed to, and no longer plagued by, their company. At night, after his usual walk with Angel, he sat on the front porch and listened to his eccentric neighbors bicker. The professor was starting to see a different side of Buddy and Clover's relationship. He found they were, and this would be a substantial understatement, oddly sportive to each other, rather than hatefully malicious, as was his initial conclusion. Yes, he could see putting green food coloring in your friend's soft drink before a date as "just joshing" a buddy. But, making a trap door for your neighbor to fall through was a bit much, even if Buddy did go over the next morning to repair the hole.

On this particular evening, the professor learned more. They grew up together and always had a brother-like relationship; it was okay for them to wreak havoc on each other, but not for anyone else. They were both life-long bachelors, both claiming, of course, that it was because of the company they kept. The professor sensed there was something more to the story. Angel concurred.

"So, professor," Buddy began, "anymore run-ins with…?" He preferred not to say the name.

"Yesterday," the professor answered.

"Are you crazy?" Clover shouted from the other porch. "Did you hear a word we said?"

"Look, this whole situation…something isn't right. There's this mysterious man who shows up at my wife's funeral, somehow knowing things that he shouldn't know. He tells me to meet him at Front Street, replaces two worn out rocking chairs with new ones and talks to me about God."

"About God?" Buddy and Clover asked in unison.

"Is he some kind of religious nut?"

Buddy and Clover thought for a few moments. "It wouldn't surprise me if he was in some cult," Buddy answered.

"Regardless," the professor chimed in, "somebody's playing a sick joke and I'm not going to be some naïve dit-dot who falls for local legend hogwash."

Buddy and Clover looked over at each other.

"What are you guys not telling me?"

"Nothing," Clover said, obviously bothered by his answer.

The professor pushed further. "If you guys know something and you're not telling me…" The professor stopped short and turned his head to look at both men. "At least consider Angel's safety."

"I can take care of myself." Angel closed the journal she was reading and joined the conversation. "Let's stop acting like children and go with Grandpa to meet him."

Clover stood quickly, causing his rocker to bounce back and forth. "You do what you've gotta do. I don't intend to get anywhere close to that madman."

"That includes me," agreed Buddy. "Listen to us, that man may talk and look like a saint, but I'm telling you, he's just plain evil."

The three men sat idle on their dimly lit porches and looked out into the thick shroud of darkness that allowed any predacious animal, or person, if indeed they were not the same, to see them without the slightest unveiling. The usual harmonious orchestra of late summer-night insects became quiet and still. Buddy and Clover were uncomfortable and sensitive to every crackle and whisper of wind. They sat, chilled in spite of the sticky humidity, wondering if he, the one neither of them liked to mention aloud, was out there, watching, planning, or ready to make true on a promise he gave them long ago, before the child incident.

"He threatened us," Clover finally blurted out. "We were hunting one day and we saw him; happened by his camp on accident. He was terrifying, his eyes all wild and crazy."

"We just turned and walked away," said Buddy. "He followed us, but we didn't dare turn around. He was right behind us, right on our heels. We could hear the breaking of branches as he tore them from the trees and bushes and tossed them at the back of our feet. Finally, he stopped and spoke, his voice was as dark as his eyes. He said he'd put an end to us if we ever came anywhere close to him again."

"He called our names. He knew who we were," Clover added, his eyes and ears sensitive to any sound or movement in the darkness.

"When we returned home from Florida, we found something that we didn't want to see." Clover again looked out into the night. "We don't trust the night. Not since he's been back. You shouldn't either."

"What did you see?" the professor asked.

"Footprints, going to each window, around both our houses. And, not only that, there were also small piles of broken branches," Clover answered. "He has this thing with branches, always carries one around, breaking it into pieces. I guess it's some sort of nervous habit."

"Whoever it was could have easily broken in if they wanted," Buddy added while chewing on his thumbnail. "They didn't want to break in. They wanted to see who was inside."

"He's just crazy," said Clover. "I don't know what he wants with us and I don't know what he wants with you, but it can't be anything good."

Buddy and Clover walked back into their houses without saying goodnight. The professor remained in his rocker. A cool summer wind brought a brief chill while the sound of deadbolts from Buddy and Clover's doors echoed into the evening. The professor stood and peered out into the darkness. He did this for a long while until he became overly perceptive to the noises of the coastal night. He walked back inside and, for the first time since he had arrived in Beaufort, he locked his door.

Chapter 10

After much debate and concessions, the professor and Angel came to an agreement: she would not go out alone at night and was never, for any reason, to go near Front Street at the sunset hour or after. She agreed, although not pleased with the feeling she was being treated like a child again. The professor exhibited a nervousness that worried her. Therefore, she relinquished her rights without any further argument.

It was late morning, on a Monday, that Angel found herself on the front porch, doing something completely unexpected and new. She was using her very own neuro- psychology techniques on herself. "You don't need the love of anyone besides yourself," she repeated, while tapping her fingers against her temples. She had discovered, during her research, that tapping on certain parts of the head could stimulate brain function, essentially retraining the subconscious mind. Doing this, while speaking affirmations aloud, enabled the brain to truly accept the spoken word and then, through "supra-conscious" workings, make anything you think or speak with certainty and most important, clarity, become your reality. Angel's research was groundbreaking in that she moved past the "sub-" conscious brain model and found something infinitely more powerful – the "supra-" conscious brain.

Angel discovered that the supraconscious mind allows everything around a person to work in their favor to reach a clearly visualized goal. And when Angel said everything, she meant…everything. *"Some of you will refer to it as the 'universe' or 'innate intelligence' and others, like myself, will call it God's created universal power, which we can all tap into, if we so desire and believe,"* she often said during her introductions.

Some people in the study, by using Angel's techniques, went on to quit smoking after a lifetime addiction, lose weight and keep it off, increase their confidence in public speaking and become more respected and better compensated in their place of work. One lady, an outsider in her town, was able to win the office of mayor, even after spending time in prison for identity thief.

"Remember," Angel always said at the end of her training sessions, *"you are not bodies walking around with brains; you are brains walking around with bodies. You've got to constantly feed your brain positive messages, and allow it to work for you, or the negative world will, without you even knowing it, control your subconscious mind and lead you toward your insecurities, fears and, ultimately, failure. The subconscious mind is no match for the supra-conscious mind. But, it's up to you to learn how to use it. That's why I'm here."*

Angel's concentration was broken when she heard a muffled voice from somewhere behind her.

"Louise cannot resist cooking for me. Louise cannot resist cooking for me. Louise cannot resist cooking for me…" Buddy was repeating his own positive affirmations while tapping, much harder than necessary, on the top of his head. When he finally opened his eyes, he found Angel staring at him with a look of displeasure on her face. Buddy ignored her obvious disproval and closed his eyes again. "Louise cannot stand cooking for Clover. Louise cannot stand cooking for Clover…"

James Graham

"It doesn't work that way," Angel finally said. "It only works on you, not someone else."

"Well, what good is that?" Buddy asked.

Angel, in frustration, placed her head in her hands. "Never mind."

"The professor told me about your work. I told him that something like that could maybe help me. But, I'm not sure he believes in all that psychic stuff."

"It's psychology, not psychic," Angel corrected him.

"Well, whatever it is, he said it probably wouldn't help me. Said I was missing some of the necessary hardware. I know what that means. It's a nice way of saying 'don't waste your time with that hocus-pocus'."

Angel rolled down the ramp and headed to Ann Street. It was a particularly noisy yet, still serene, morning. The baby birds were pleading with their mother for just one more worm. Even the sound of bumblebees romancing the Yellow Jessamine added to the grandeur of summer on the coast. Angel closed her eyes, but concentrated on something altogether different than usual. "I can have true love in my life. I can have true love in my life. I can have…" She would die if anyone ever learned of her new affirmation.

50

Chapter 11

The professor sat in his leather chesterfield surrounded by a small pile of books and a laptop computer, filtering through volumes of information. His library was a sacred place, a place where he could dull the pain of missing Sharon. Of course, nothing could take it all away, with the exception of ceasing to breathe. One of the things Angel taught him about grief was that the human mind could only hold one thought at a time. So, although thoughts could come and go, if you immersed yourself with a particular thought, it could give a reprieve, albeit temporary, from mental anguish. She called it a "mental band aid."

This idea seemed to be working, even as the professor thumbed through Sharon's old Bible. He found the second chapter of Genesis and led his finger to the seventh verse: "the Lord God formed the man from the dust of the ground…"

"This doesn't prove anything," the professor said to himself. He switched back to the human anatomy text and again read the list of elements that make up the human body. He then read through the index of a Geology textbook and compared the elements in the earth's crust. This is completely anecdotal, he thought. Just because the body is indeed made up of the very elements that come from the earth, doesn't mean the Bible has any great truth. Moses made a lucky guess. Besides, why not compare the body with dust, it goes well with the prose. If everything began with the same explosion, then certainly everything should have the same elements. Everything comes from the same thing - *Or does it?* the professor thought. Fish are not made of these elements. Frogs, snakes and even other mammals are not made of the same elements of the human body. In fact, maybe most things of this earth are not of the same elements found in the dirt or *dust* of the earth. So, it is interesting that the NASA scientists found the human body to have such a strong connection to earth's dust. The professor closed the books and placed them back to their rightful place among the other diverse collection of books. There were no conclusions that this meant anything. Maybe it did have some relevance to Biblical truth. But, then, maybe it did not. The professor kept his faith that it meant absolutely nothing.

He then flipped a few more pages and found the seventh chapter and verses seventeen through twenty: "For forty days the flood kept coming on the earth, and as the waters increased they lifted the ark high above the earth. The waters rose and increased greatly on the earth, and the ark floated on the surface of the water. They rose greatly on the earth, and all the high mountains under the entire heavens were covered. The waters rose and covered the mountains to a depth of more than twenty feet." He then turned the pages to the eighth chapter and fourth verse: "...and on the seventeenth day of the seventh month the ark came to rest on the mountains of Ararat."

The professor gave off a grunt as he finished reading the verses. This was, all things considered, an interesting coincidence. But he suspected there was more to the story than what Timothy Lee revealed. He opened his laptop and began searching the web for Mount Ararat and Noah's Ark.

About an hour had passed when the professor closed the computer and lit a cigar. He stretched back into the chesterfield and blew a circle of smoke in the air. He was almost pleased with himself and his discerning eye. The strange object at the top of Mount Ararat has never reached a fruition of truth that it was, in fact, the Biblical ark. It likely never will. And, as for the seashells on mountaintops – they too, the professor discovered, could not be conclusive evidence of the Biblical flood. He, in fact, felt almost foolish that he ever found the fact of interest. Every scientist knows that mountains form when two or more of the earth's plates collide together. It is like pushing two rugs together, causing them to crumple upward. If this happened slowly, it certainly would not explain how seashells found their way to the mountain peaks. However, if a cataclysmic earthquake caused two plates to crush together with a particularly violent force, it could cause mountains to form rather quickly. And if those two plates happen to be beneath the ocean at that time, it would explain how seashells and sea creatures found themselves on mountain peaks. Essentially, the ocean floor became a mountain in a matter of minutes. Even in modern times, mountain peaks have grown after earthquakes. In May of 2008, a 7.9 magnitude earthquake in China caused the Longmenshan fault system of the Himalaya Mountains to crush together causing a block of earth to thrust upward. This collision caused the western Himalayas to rise higher.

"Indeed, things are not always what they seem," the professor said to himself. He was almost content for that short moment in time. But, when his eyes came across a picture of Sharon, he crushed the cigar in an ashtray and placed his hands over his face. The faint sound of weeping echoed down the hallway.

Chapter 12

When Angel arrived at the church, she noticed a group of people walking through the old cemetery with a guide. She immediately recognized Jack's voice.

As he received his last tip, Jack spoke briefly with the remaining visitors. When he turned to walk back in the church, he saw Angel sitting at the top of the ramp.

"Well, that's strange," he said. "I was just thinking about you and here you are."

"That's not so strange. It's called the law of attraction."

Jack blushed and was embarrassed to do so.

"No, silly. Not that kind of attraction. Let's get out of the heat and I'll show you."

Jack, still blushing, opened the door for Angel and entered the nicely cooled sanctuary. "So, now that I've flattered myself, tell me about this law of attraction."

Angel looked around the church and set her eyes on two pianos. One was located at the front of the church and the other was about fifty yards away near the back rows of the sanctuary.

"The law of attraction states that we unknowingly send out resonations or vibrations that attract similar people or whatever we knowingly, or unknowingly, think about. This can be a positive power or a negative power. Keep in mind that this law only pertains to the person using it. So, you can't attract something to another person, only to yourself."

Jack lifted his brows. "Sounds a little bit out there to me. And here I was thinking you would find me a little strange."

"Well, you do give tours through a creepy graveyard," Angel shot back.

Jack laughed and shook his head in agreement. "That does sound weird when you put it that way."

Angel also laughed. "Put it that way? How else do you put it?"

"I don't know. Maybe see it as being kindhearted. Those people have been buried since the seventeen hundreds. You could get really bored lying around that long. I, as a compassionate young man, like to think I keep them company and bring visitors to…well, visit."

"Yeah, sure," Angel said sarcastically. "Now, back to your lesson on the law of attraction. You say it sounds out there, but consider this: have you ever found yourself thinking about someone that you haven't seen or spoken to in years and out of nowhere they call or you see them out somewhere?"

Jack thought about it. "Well, yeah."

"And I bet this has happened more than once. In fact, it has probably happened dozens of times."

"So I'm sending 'vibrations' out to these people?"

"Precisely," Angel answered confidently. "But, you're still not convinced and do you know why?"

"Why?"

"Because you're a man."

"Oh really? Well, I may not be a brain expert but I happen to know that it's a scientific fact that women have thicker skulls than men."

Angel enjoyed the volley. "Men do have thinner skulls, which is precisely why they can't keep anything in there."

Jack laughed and gave a playful push on Angels shoulder. She became quiet and, as silly as it was, almost bashful.

"Did I do something?" Jack asked.

Angel shook her head. "No, I just thought about something. But, it's nothing."

Angel had never laughed with a friend before, as difficult as that was to believe. When Jack playfully touched her shoulder, it felt different. It felt strangely good. She was enjoying herself. She wasn't thinking about her goals or how much she needed to exercise her legs. She was only thinking about the present. It was silly. She was a mature young lady, she told herself. But, the reality was still there. Jack was her friend. And, as she thought back, she had never taken the time to make friends.

"What do you say you come back tonight and I'll give you a private tour of the old burying ground by candle light?"

Angel was back in the moment. "Sounds like a…" She stopped herself before finishing the sentence. Certainly she couldn't say "date." Jack was a friend, a buddy, nothing else.

"Well?" Jack waited for an answer.

"First you have to humor me."

"Okay. A man walks into a church with a parrot on his shoulder…"

"No, silly, not a joke. It's called the law of sympathetic resonance." Angel rolled over to the baby grand piano. She pointed inside at one of the chords. "See this? This is the G chord. I'm going over to the other piano and will push the G key on it. All I need is for you to keep an eye on this chord. Understand?"

"Gotcha."

Angel pushed her way up the slopped aisle and moved the stool from the front of the older piano.

"Are you watching?" she asked when she caught Jack staring at her.

"I'm watching."

Angel pushed the G key and allowed it to quietly echo through the back room. "Anything happening?" she spoke loudly so Jack could hear her.

Jack watched the chord carefully. "It's vibrating," he finally said.

"Are any of the other chords *vibrating*?"

Jack smiled as he watched the lone chord vibrate. "Only the G chord," he answered.

"Just to prove the point, I want you to pick any chord you would like. Just give me the number."

Jack studied the other chords before answering. "The sixth one to the right."

Angel counted and then pushed the key. Jack was amazed to see that specific chord vibrate.

"Let me guess," Angel spoke at the top of her voice, "the chord is *resonating*?"

"It's resonating," Jack conceded.

Angel rolled back to the front and began playing a short note on the piano. "The law of attraction is caused, in part, by the law of sympathetic resonance. When you broke into this church, the wrong people were influencing you. But, you thought that was the company you should be around because you thought you weren't good enough to fit in with any other kind of people."

"You don't have to be so…"

"Truthful? You're a good person Jack. The only one in this room that doesn't think so is you. And when you think that way you will attract that kind of people and that kind of life to yourself."

"I come from dirt," Jack admitted, not even trying to conceal the fact. "Around here when you come from dirt you stay with dirt. Nobody else will accept you, no matter what you do."

"If you're worried about what other people think of you, you'll probably be offended to learn how little they actually do think about you."

Jack wanted to change the subject. He had been feeling so happy and now he found himself back to his reality. "So, are we still on for tonight?"

"You'll have to come get me."

"You mean go to your house?" Jack knew that his kind did not belong around her neighborhood. "Yes, my house. I'm not allowed out after dark by myself."

"How old are you?" Jack asked.

"You know you shouldn't ask a lady her age."

He liked the way Angel made him feel. He liked that someone really wanted to take the effort to be around him. He liked being liked.

"What's the address?"

Chapter 13

When Angel returned to the cottage, she found an envelope slid under the door. On it, in childlike handwriting, was simply "professor". She found her grandfather asleep in his rocker with an opened book across his lap.

"Grandpa," she whispered.

The professor opened his eyes to find Angel beside him, holding the envelope in her right hand. "For me?"

"I found it under the door."

The professor took the envelope and carefully opened it. Inside was a note.

Dear professor,

Let's meet after dark. It's a special night.

Timothy Lee

"Is it from him? Was he here? " Angel asked.

"If I don't go to him, he's going to come to us. I'll be fine. Remember our agreement."

"Grandpa, I'm worried about you going down there by yourself. What if he hurts you?"

"Angel, you know how these people are. I have to follow his wishes until I can figure out a way to get the police involved. We can't risk angering him without knowing, for sure, that he won't be able to retaliate."

"I don't like this at all," Angel said as she held the professor's hand.

"You just stay put and don't go down there."

"I'm meeting Jack tonight. He's coming here to get me."

"He's coming here? I don't want him in this house. He can wait outside. Understand?" The professor was not happy with the idea of a troubled young man coming to his house, especially not to take his granddaughter out at night. But, he knew he could not keep her from the world forever. "Keep your cell phone on and call me."

Clover looked both ways to ensure no one could see him. The road was empty and there were no people walking the sidewalks of Ann Street. He looked back at Mrs. Jean's beautiful flowers. She was a meticulous gardener; had been for over seventy years. No matter how hot and humid it was, you could always find her in her oversized sun hat, pulling weeds and watering her garden of roses, sun-flowers and a host of lilies.

Mrs. Jean became a regional celebrity after discovering a new species of lily in the sand hills of eastern North Carolina. The "Sandhills Lily" became the official name of the three-foot high, yellow and orange flower. Mrs. Jean donated her most beautiful lily to the Herbarium at the University of North

Carolina at Chapel Hill. Botany lovers from across the nation came to see the new lily. Many people made the three and a half hour trip from Chapel Hill to Beaufort to meet the woman who grew the first of the species and possessed, arguably, the largest and most beautiful lily garden in the world.

Mrs. Jean was a wonderfully sweet lady – as long as you did not touch her lilies. Everyone in Beaufort knew better than to make that mistake.

But, Clover was hungry for Louise's chicken and dumplings. And when Clover got food on his mind, he was fully willing to risk his life for it. He knew a sure fire way to get at least a week's rations was to bring Louise one of the world's rarest and most cherished gifts: a marble-filled crystal vase adorned with a foot-long, orange-yellow Sandhill lily.

Clover checked the road again. It was clear. He pulled the camouflage hat down to conceal his eyes and grasped the fine-toothed steak knife.

When he was younger, folks called Clover the "gray squirrel" because of his rodent-like quickness and the gray blur of his pasty skin as he easily outran every first grader at Beaufort Elementary. He said the secret was in the way he chopped his hands, but most of the first graders felt it was because he was in the sixth grade. Regardless, Clover was confident that given the right circumstances, he could still live up to that name. So, with his hands chopping and a Sandhill lily in his mouth, he did just that.

Across the street from Mrs. Jean's house, a bush of Azaleas jostled loudly. Buddy cleared the branches from his head and shoulders and stood from his cover. He smiled as he watched the "gray squirrel" disappear around the Moore Street corner.

He then took a bite from an apple and looked down at a camera in his hand. After reviewing the digital picture of Clover stealing Mrs. Jean's lily, he laughed loudly and walked home.

Chapter 14

Angel stared in the mirror and repeated her affirmations. "I can have love in my life. I can have true love. I can have this." It wasn't so much that she wanted Jack's love, at least not specifically. Besides, she really did not know that much about him. What she did know was that for the first time in her life, she had *perfect clarity* of what she was missing. She knew the risk of love included losing it, almost assuredly, at some point. She witnessed it firsthand as she watched her grandfather become grieved and lonesome. In her mind, after considering the possibilities, love was worth its price. And its price was the unspeakable pain that followed its loss.

When the doorbell rang, Angel tweaked her lipstick once more and then wheeled through the living room. She took a deep breath, said one more affirmation and opened the door. Jack was handsome, standing with a single rose, his hand shaking as he handed it to Angel.

"Thank you. I didn't know we were giving gifts."

Jack's smile was more than enough of a gift. Of course, Angel would never say that. That would make her vulnerable, and she was not ready to go there yet.

"You look awful nice to be going to a graveyard," Jack said.

"And you smell awful to be going anywhere," Angel said, fanning Jack's cheap cologne from her nose.

Jack was embarrassed. Doug, one of the volunteers at the church, chided him earlier about keeping animals away with his cologne. "My Lord, son." Doug said. "My eyes are a burning. Did you splash it on or take a bath in it?"

Jack had never used cologne before and he told himself he never would again. Angel grabbed Jack's hand and apologized for being rude. "I expect nothing less from a city girl," he said. They both laughed and made their way out the door and to the church.

Angel kept wiping her eyes as they traveled down Ann Street. "Allergies?" Jack asked. They both laughed, again. Angel smiled to herself. She forgot all about her affirmations. Jack forgot about his terrible life.

The professor struggled to see through the darkness as he turned right on Ann Street and walked toward the west end. He could usually see the stranger by now, but in the dark of night, he was unsure of every shadow he came across. When he got within ten yards of the meeting place, he was finally able to focus and see Timothy Lee.

"Professor, so glad you could make it. Welcome back. It won't be long now. I know you can't wait to see Sharon again."

The professor was over the anger he had initially when the stranger spoke of Sharon. Now, he just blocked it out, knowing it was best to play along with this obviously disturbed individual. Sharon was dead and at peace. The professor was just waiting for his turn.

"A telescope," the professor said after examining the instrument in front of his rocking chair.

"I just love the solar system," Timothy Lee said with the excitement of a child. "Do you study the stars at all, professor?"

The professor took a moment to peer through the scope before answering without enthusiasm, "I do."

"Well, great! We should have a lot to talk about." The stranger was overly excited about the evening's plans.

The professor had read up on mental illnesses, including schizophrenia, and noticed that Timothy Lee was exhibiting textbook symptoms of the condition. But, from a purely visible standpoint, the stranger looked so…well, pleasant. In addition, with the exception of his current behavior, he always seemed wise and intellectually persuasive. The professor again studied Timothy Lee's appearance. He was a fairly young man, no older than forty-five. His curly brown hair was well trained, without a single strand out of place. His face was smooth with freshly shaved cheeks that showcased eyes of piercing, deep green. His expression was alluring and, yet, tranquil. A persistent smile dominated the right side of his mouth and a faint sparkle made its home in his right eye, as well. Even his impeccably trimmed eyebrows were cared for with the utmost attention. From the outside, if you did not know Timothy Lee, or his history, you would think he was on the road to becoming an influential, small town politician. Instead, he was one of the mentally unstable people whom no one expected of doing whatever nasty deed he or she had done.

Timothy Lee slid in front of the telescope and began observing the beauty of the constellations that only a dark, yet clear, night could offer. "Oh, professor, it's a beauty up there tonight."

The professor placed his hands in his pocket and briefly skimmed the night sky.

"Isn't it amazing how perfectly tuned this solar system is?" Timothy Lee made a slight adjustment to his gaze.

The professor wanted nothing more than to end the night, but he knew he had to play along. "I guess," he was only able to reply.

"I mean, if we were just a wee bit closer to the sun, the earth would burn and all life would end. On the other hand, if we were just a wee bit farther away we'd all freeze to death. Either way you slice, it seems we're pretty lucky to be just where we are." Timothy Lee lifted his head from the telescope. "Wouldn't you agree, professor, that we're pretty lucky?"

"Pretty lucky," he agreed.

The stranger placed his head back down and again peered through the instrument. "Do you know how fast the earth rotates?"

"I can't say I do." The professor was miserable. He wanted nothing more than to run away from Carteret County and never come back. When Sharon died, he felt that he could never leave her remains. But, with this mysterious stranger running his life, he felt that leaving her was his only chance to look back and enjoy her.

"One thousand and two miles per hour. That's the speed it takes the earth to rotate once every twenty-four hours."

Both men were quiet for a few moments before Timothy Lee spoke again. "That speed is precisely what is needed to balance out the earth's gravity. So, professor, if we ever start spinning just a wee bit faster, everything, including the earth and us, would fly off into space. We'd all die in that beautiful black abyss. On the other hand, if the earth, for whatever reason, ever slowed down just the slightest, everything would suck in and implode into complete and utter destruction. Not a thing on earth would survive."

The professor's patience was growing thin. "Look, Timothy…"

"Timothy Lee."

"Timothy Lee then. I'm really enjoying your little galaxy lecture, but isn't there something else you want with me?"

"Professor," the man began with a tone of deep sincerity, "I know what you're thinking and I assure you, I'm not here to add misery to your misery. I only come to help. I want to show you how you can see your wife again. She wants to show you that she's okay."

The professor became more impatient with his company. "I need to go. Maybe we can talk at some other time."

Timothy Lee only smiled. "Do you know how much the earth is tilted?"

"I don't care what…"

"Twenty-three degrees. That's precisely the angle of tilt we need to allow the earth to remain inhabitable. Without that precise tilt, half of the earth would not be inhabitable and half the crops would be destroyed." Timothy Lee continued smiling at the professor. "We'd get pretty hungry, professor. And then we'd die."

"Look, enough of this. I don't want to upset you, but you need help and I will help you get it if you would just leave me and my daughter alone."

"You mean Angel? She's such an interesting study."

An interesting study, the professor repeated the words to himself, words he had heard Angel say hundreds of times about her studies – *Jack is an interesting study.* "Where did you get that from?" The professor's anger was growing to a breaking point. "How do you know her words you…"

"Professor, do you know why it's a special night?"

The professor's voice became loud and aggressive, "Look… you…I don't care why this night is special…"

"Seventy years ago," Timothy stopped and looked at his watch. "Seventy years ago, at this exact time, Beverly was born, just as it was planned. Just as the earth's rotation, its distance from the sun and its tilt were planned out. Professor," the stranger's smile broadened, "almost everything is planned, maybe even you meeting me."

The professor was again speechless. He knew this date and he knew the time of her birth. But, nobody else should know, or even care for that matter.

Timothy Lee sat back down and looked through the telescope. He rotated it to the north and then stood up and faced the professor. "Before I go, would you like to take a look through my telescope?"

The professor was still in shock. "No thank you," he said through his fog.

"Professor, I'm asking you to look. I would like you to look."

The professor, insensate, walked slowly to the telescope and looked through the lens. Timothy Lee then rotated the scope to the right. "What do you see here professor?"

"The big dipper," he answered.

The stranger turned the scope a little farther. "And here?"

"Little dipper."

"And here?"

"Orion."

"Here?"

"Cygnus."

"Excellent. And here?"

"Gemini."

"Here?"

"Scorpius."

"Very impressive, professor. You really are a star man. How about one more?"

Timothy Lee turned the telescope to the north and held it firm. Here, professor, what do you see here?"

The professor looked through the telescope but was unable to see anything.

"Any stars, professor?"

The professor continued his search in vain. "I don't see any stars."

"Anything at all, professor?"

"There's nothing."

"Nothing?" Timothy Lee repeated. "You mean it's an *empty space*? No stars? No constellations? Nothing?"

The professor lifted his head and looked up at the north sky, trying to view the empty space.

"You can't see it with the naked eye. It has only been in recent years, with the invention of these powerful telescopes, that scientists have found this strange area. It's an *empty space* - nothing."

The professor looked again through the telescope and studied the odd, empty space in the north sky.

"It's a huge hole in space, professor. Just north of the earth axis...empty."

The professor rubbed his eyes. He was exhausted both mentally and physically. He wanted nothing more than to have peace in his life, some time to mourn the loss of his wife and reflect upon what to do with the rest of his own life. Instead, he felt trapped by a Bible toting madman who opened old wounds and had him fighting off the ridiculous thought that he may actually be able to see his wife again.

Timothy Lee placed his hand upon the professor's shoulder. His touch was gentle and caring. His voice was also kind. "Why don't you go home and get some sleep. Can we meet tomorrow, at sunset?" He took a moment to let the professor think. "I really am here to help. I don't mean to cause you any additional anguish."

The professor felt dizzy with confusion. He felt weak, defeated, and unsure if anything was real. Was it he who was losing his bearings?

Timothy Lee handed the professor a picture. "It's a souvenir, a picture of the empty place in space. You have something in common with that place, don't you?"

The professor struggled to see the picture in the dark, but was able to make out most of it.

"I hope you're enjoying the verses." Timothy Lee knew that was not the case. "Job 26:7. It's an interesting little verse. It was written 3500 years ago, long before these fancy telescopes came about. I think it's important that you remember that – *nobody could see this empty place 3500 years ago* because they didn't have the technology. And, yet, somehow they knew it was there."

"What are you talking about?" the professor asked, confused by the tiresome riddle.

Timothy Lee smiled and gazed up at the night sky. "Goodnight, Professor."

The professor walked back to the cottage, in the dark, thinking about so much – but mostly about seventy years ago that night.

As the professor turned to walk up his steps, he noticed his mailbox had a magazine stuffed in it, keeping the lid jarred open. He pulled the magazine out and sat in his rocker, allowing the yellow glow of the porch light to illuminate the cover. It was Science Magazine, a journal the professor knew well. The cover felt rigid and new like a fresh playing card.

This is odd, the professor thought as he noticed the date. Like the *Washington Times* newspaper Timothy Lee left before, this magazine was also old by its date, but not its appearance.

"November twenty-seventh, nineteen eighty-one," the professor read with a low voice. He noticed a page folded halfway through the magazine. He opened it and read the article headline: "Delving the Hole in Space." The professor ran his finger down until he reached an underlined sentence. He read it with a whisper. "The recently announced 'hole in space', a 300 million light year gap in the distribution of galaxies, has taken cosmologists by surprise..."

The professor found a note scribbled in the outside column. "Professor, not everyone was surprised by this. It's old news – 3500 years old news. How did the Bible know about this hole in space without today's telescopes? Just something to think about – that's all. T.L."

The professor walked quickly into the house and opened Sharon's Bible to Job 26:7. He read the verse to himself and then walked to the window. After he spread the curtains apart he looked up at the stars and, if only softly, chuckled.

Chapter 15

Jack struggled with the padlock and chain that secured the rustic iron-gate leading into the old burying ground. Angel sat quietly behind him, not sure if she liked the way the old live oak trees crept back and forth with the sea breeze. The long, timeworn limbs of the oaks traveled away from the trunk and lolled just a few feet above the ground. With each breeze, the outer branches became mildly aroused from their ancient slumber but quickly fell back to their preferred resting place as soon as the breeze had passed.

Jack released the rusted chain and opened the creaking gate. "You ready?"

Angel looked around at the ancient burying ground and its oak guardians. "I think I would enjoy this more in the daylight."

"Don't tell me you're scared," Jacked chided. He then kneeled down on one knee to look Angel in the eyes. "The burying ground has always been more active at night."

Angel disliked it when people knelt down to talk to her. It made her feel disabled and different. She especially disliked it when Jack did this. "There are more breezes at night," Angel responded. "That's why it seems more active."

Jack lifted an eyebrow as he considered this fact. "That's your theory." He then put on his best scary face, his eyes wide and mysterious, which he had done so many times with his tour groups.

Angel pretended to ignore the look and pushed her wheelchair through the gate, barely able to fit through without crushing her fingers. She noticed the ground was bare and, unlike the rest of downtown Beaufort, completely void of grass. The dirt ground was covered with oak shells that crackled like cheap candy wrappers as Angel moved farther into the cemetery.

Jack lit an old oil lamp and moved in front of Angel. "Back here," he pointed to the northwest corner. "It appears empty, but you're actually rolling over bundles of graves. This wasn't known until 1992 when an archaeological survey found it was full of unmarked graves. The bodies had their scalps cleft, something that likely happened in 1711 when Coree and Neusiok Indians whipped out most of the early Beaufort population."

"Isn't it disrespectful for you to walk across these graves?"

Jack's eyes got big and dark, again using the scary face he had performed repeatedly during his tours. "Yes it is. Trust me. I know this from experience. After walking over these graves, people have claimed to be startled from their sleep by the sound of Indian's chanting during the darkest hour of night. Some people have even awakened to find clumps of hair on their pillows." Jack again widened his eyes like a masterful storyteller. "It's true," he whispered.

"Are you serious?" Angel asked, not believing a word Jack said.

Jack again widened his eyes, this time like a vampire before biting his victim. "No."

Angel laughed. "You're going to make a great father."

Jack liked the way she said this. "You really think so?"

"I do."

Jack let the compliment settle in before moving on with his tour. "So, these graves all face east. This, as legend tells it, is so those buried here can face the sun when they are risen on "Judgment Morn."

"Creepy," Angel said.

"Not nearly as creepy as this," Jack replied. "This is a grave of a little English girl. She came to Beaufort as an infant when her parents moved away from England. She wanted to see her homeland so much that she pleaded with her mother to allow her to journey back. With time, the little girl persuaded her mother to allow her to go. But, the mother would only allow this if the father went with her and promised to bring her back in one piece. So, the little girl and her father made the trip to England but, tragically, the little girl died on the trip back to Beaufort. In those days when someone died aboard a ship, far from land, they were buried at sea so the body didn't decompose on the ship. The father was devastated and couldn't stand the idea of throwing his little girl into the cold ocean, so he purchased a keg of rum from the ship cargo. He then placed his little girl in the rum, sealed it back to preserve her and brought her back to Beaufort where she was buried, right here, in a keg of rum."

Jack again widened his eyes with his best scary look, but this time he could not stay serious and instead began laughing at himself. Angel laughed along with him.

"I can't believe I'm laughing at you when a poor child is buried here."

"I agree, you're sick," Jack said before widening his eyes again. Angel could not help but laugh at his antics.

"This is the worst tour group I have ever had," Jack said jokingly. "Let's move on." He pushed Angel through the dirt pathways that meandered through the ancient graves. The oak trees swayed back and forth as an occasional gust of wind whistled through the decrepit branches.

"This place really is kind of creepy," Angel said.

"I used to think so too, but now I really like it here. This is one place where you can really get away. Nobody comes in an iron gated graveyard in the twilight, much less after sunset."

"You really come in here alone? At night?"

"I'll show you my favorite place." Jack continued pushing Angel's wheelchair until they stopped in front of a peculiar looking gravesite. On top of the grave was a large steel cannon. "His name was Captain Otway Burns. He was a hero during the War of 1812. His ship was the Snap Dragon and this is one of the cannons from that very ship."

Angel wheeled to the side of the cannon and ran her hand along its cold, smooth surface. "And why exactly do you like this one?"

"May I show you?"

"That's why I asked."

"Can you...is it okay if I...if you can, maybe...sit on the cannon?" Jack stuttered his words, trying his best not to offend Angel.

Angel thought about how awkward it would be to have Jack help her up, but also how it would seem even more uncomfortable and handicapped to say no. "I just need a little support."

Jack felt very unsure as he placed Angel's arm around his neck and helped her stand. He was surprised at how well she did once she was up. As she supported herself on Jack's shoulder, she was very calculated as she stepped, noticeably unbalanced, toward the cannon.

Angel took her arm away from Jack's shoulder and placed it, along with the other, on the cannon. She stood for a moment until her shaky legs became more sturdy and then turned to face Jack, allowing the cannon to hold her upright from behind.

Jack wanted to comment on how great she did, but knew Angel did not like being patronized in any way, especially by her handicap.

As Angel stood, facing Jack, she studied his face. It was pleasant, she thought. She noticed his long bangs were trimmed, no longer hanging over his right eye.

"You got a haircut?"

Jack stood defensively, not sure if he needed to be in place to catch Angel if she lost balance. He continued looking at her waist, unknowingly swaying as his eyes followed her torso. Angel removed a hand from the cannon and used it to lift Jack's chin until his eyes met hers.

"I'm okay. I won't fall."

Jack stood, facing Angel, his hands a few inches away from each side of her waist. He was somewhat embarrassed and quickly moved his hands away from her. "I'm sorry, I…"

"It's fine," Angel cut him off. "You got a haircut. It looks nice."

"Got tired of blowing hair off from my eyes."

"You have a nice face. You shouldn't cover it with long bangs."

Jack and Angel became uncomfortable and quickly changed the subject.

"Can you sit up here?" Jack asked, motioning to the cannon.

"Sure, just give me a lift."

Jack was unsure of how he should help Angel. He stepped towards her and then away to study the situation.

"Just boost me up by my waist," Angel instructed him.

Jack made sure Angel was secure on the cannon and then jumped up beside her. The sea breeze picked up and made the long tree limbs wave back and forth, groaning with each sway.

Angel looked around before saying, "What do you like so much about sitting on this grave?"

"I don't enjoy sitting," Jack began. "I enjoy laying on it."

Angel looked up to see what the view would be like on her back. She noticed the large opening through the trees that gave a clear view of the night sky.

"You wanna try?" Jack asked.

"Sure."

Jack slid off the cannon and stood close as Angel carefully found a position on her back. She did not say a word as she looked through the opening of the live oaks.

"What do you think?" Jack asked, after a moment of silence.

"It's beautiful, Jack. It really is. It makes you forget all about being in a graveyard."

"I feel like I'm part of history when I lay here, almost as if I know Captain Otway and nobody else does."

"It makes you forget," Angel added. "It lets you escape from the now."

Jack sat down and leaned his back against the grave. "Yeah, the Captain and I have had a lot of talks."

Angel looked down at Jack. "I'm sure he enjoys them as much as I do."

Chapter 16

A warm breeze rolled across Front Street, the final chore of the retiring sun. The border of the great star began to blur as orange and pink strands weaved their way through the paper-thin clouds. Across from Taylor's Creek, wild horses grazed and enjoyed the peacefulness that always accompanied the re-treating hours of summer days. The professor sat alone in one of the rockers, his eyes closed as he reminisced about the walks he took with Sharon. He remembered them well: holding hands, remarking about the beauty all around them. Front Street was a special place, a familiar place. It was Sharon's childhood playground. The professor envisioned her, young and innocent, and wished that he could have been in her life during those years, too. It was certainly a selfish wish, he thought. He had so many of her good years. Everybody needs different chapters, at least during the early years. What is most important, the professor was quite certain, is whom you end the story with. His ended with Sharon's death, although bur-ied somewhere deep inside was the unspoken hope that he really could see her again. If only the stranger was right, and the professor could see her – just one more time, just for a moment. But, that possibility was completely illogical and, by all physical and natural laws, impossible. A desperate, broken heart can make a person do, or hope for, impossible things.

The professor lifted his head and breathed deeply, tasting the salt air, seasoned perfectly by summer's pollination. He realized that he was beginning to feel out of place. It was as if he had suddenly outstayed his welcome. Sharon had been gone for weeks. He could only liken the feeling to going to a friend's house for the summer, but the friend had to go away early. And yet, you stayed. It felt strange. He had no other family in Beaufort. Angel would be there for only another month, two at most, depending on which school gave her the best offer. After she left, it would be only he. Well, there was Clover and Buddy. But, they were not family. They were simply an escape from reality. Even they could not be around forever. As for Timothy Lee, he would hopefully be back in a psyche ward soon. The professor chuckled to himself. *Then I'll really be alone,* he thought. *Just a petulant old man waiting to die.*

The professor rocked back in his chair and noticed a family walking along the seawall in front of him. It was obviously two young parents with their three children in tow. The big brother knelt down and began showing his two younger sisters something on the shore.

"See those little crabs?" the young boy began. His little sisters were much too young to converse back, certainly no older than two years. Yet, they were none-the-less captivated by their older brother's story.

The two girls, they appeared to be twins, peered down at the fiddler crabs as they scurried about.

"Now, when I throw this shell in the mud, I have them trained to run into the nearest hole. Then I'll count to five, slowly, and they will start coming back out." The boy stood and smiled back at his parents. His mother grabbed his father's hand and smiled. Her smile was beautiful. It reminded the professor of Sharon's smile. *Dear God, he missed that smile.*

The young boy threw the shell in the mud, causing the crabs to run for shelter. He then began counting and, sure enough, after a count of five the fiddler crabs began shuffling out of their holes and back into their frenzied world. The two toddlers clapped and cheered. The boy was obviously pleased with himself. Nevertheless, as the girls cooed and tottered in the carriage, the boy noticed the professor sitting by himself, lost in the scene. The child walked up to the apparently troubled man and held out his hand to shake. "I'm Dillon Robbins. What's your name?"

The young boy's candor caught the professor off guard, but he quickly composed himself and answered. "I'm Mike."

The young parents followed the child and also introduced themselves. The professor could not help but stare at the mother's beautiful smile. It reminded him so much of Sharon's.

The young father also introduced himself. "I'm Chance Gordon. You said your name was Mike?"

"Mike Valentine. Nice to meet you."

Chance turned to introduce his family. "This is my wife, Wendy, and our twins Ema Grace and Leslie Sue."

The professor nodded his head in recognition.

"Do you live in Beaufort?"

"Moved here after my wife got sick. This is her hometown."

Chance had an apprehensive look on his face. "Is your wife doing better now?"

"She died. Cancer."

"We lost a friend two years ago from brain cancer. It's a terrible thing."

An awkward silence lasted for a moment, but felt much longer. The professor would typically dismiss himself when conversations lost their flavor. However, with Timothy Lee due, or actually past due, to show up, he did not want to miss another opportunity to figure out who the stranger really was.

"Well, it's been nice meeting you. If you ever want to talk, take a walk, whatever, please give me a call."

Chance handed the professor a card with his name and number on it. The professor studied it. *The Finding Life Center. Pastor Chance Gordon."*

The professor handed the card back. "I'm not much on churches."

It was then that the young boy asked the professor if he could sing him a song. Certainly, the professor could not deny such a sweet child from doing so.

"I'd love to hear your song," he replied to Dillon.

"Okay then, now I have to tell you that I didn't write this song. I copied it." He cleared his throat and then when his voice rang out, it sent shivers down the professor's spine. The child's voice was innocent and pure; a purity that fit the simplicity of the verse the child sang of *Jesus loves me.* When he finished his song, the professor thanked him earnestly and then the boy and his family said goodbye.

The professor slumped forward, placed his head in his hands and slowly rocked back and forth. Another hour had past and still no sign of Timothy Lee. He opened his hands slightly and allowed only his eyes to look ahead at the shoreline. It was a particularly busy night with the shriek of seagulls dominating the afternoon chorus. A lone pelican sat on an old wooden stake waiting for his chance to catch an afternoon meal. Its feathers were weak and untamed. The bird reminded him of himself: old, tired, and simply trying to exist, if necessary. Food was more for comfort as opposed to a means to survive. Survival was no longer a goal. Instead, it was more of a trifling chore.

A cool breeze pushed its way onshore and styled the professor's thin come-over to the opposite side. A few hairs spiked upward, refusing the uniformity of the others. He closed his eyes again and drifted away to a happier time; a time when everything in life was waiting for him and love was a beautiful and newly discovered frontier. The professor had a first love, but her name was not Sharon. It was Beverly.

Wake Forest University, Winston-Salem, NC
Forty-five years earlier…

Michael Valentine sat across from Beverly, admiring the way she sipped her coffee without moving her eyes off him. Three years earlier, as an awkward freshman, he would have never guessed she would take any prolonged interest in him, much less fall in love with him.

"Happy three-year anniversary," Michael said as he reached across the table and gently held Beverly's hands.

"The best three years of my life," Beverly replied before sitting her coffee down and giving her full attention to Michael.

Michael looked down and took a deep breath. "Look, Beverly, there's something I need to get off my chest."

Beverly smiled and nodded her head, feeling certain as to what Michael would say next. *"Is congratulations in order?"* she asked.

"Congratulations?"

"You won, didn't you? You got the Rhodes."

Beverly was referring to the Rhodes Scholarship. The scholarship, given each year to a few selected students from across the nation, paid the way for each recipient's term of study at the University of Oxford, outside of London, England.

Michael put his head down and cradled his forehead, as if trying to detain a headache. *"Well, I guess you were going to find out anyway, but that's not what I wanted to tell you."*

Beverly smiled while at the same time her eyes showed confusion.

"Beverly, look, I'm really glad we've been together this long." He looked down again, unable to look her in the eye. *"I really am…"*

"But," Beverly helped, with more concern on her face.

"But, I need a change. I need to do something different. I'm in a rut and I just can't do this anymore. I shouldn't be in this kind of a relationship. I'm sorry. I'm so sorry."

"What are you trying to say?" Beverly asked as mascara and tears streamed down her cheeks. She began crying more audibly, drawing attention from the neighboring tables. Michael returned their looks with an embarrassed 'don't worry' smile.

Beverly attempted to dry her eyes and compose herself before looking back up at Michael. *"What kind of change do you…"* she began before finding a small box in front of her. She paused for a moment and then opened it.

Michael Valentine knelt down on one knee. *"This kind of change. Will you marry me?"*

The professor stood and walked to the edge of the creek. He tried not to visit that part of his life. He kept it buried, forced from his thoughts and, most importantly, his heart. But now, after so many years, the scar was reopened and threatened to infect what life the professor had left in him.

"Where are you?" the professor whispered to himself. He looked along the shoreline and back toward the businesses. "He's crazy, anyhow," the professor groaned. He unfolded some pages that he held in his hand, briefly glanced at them, and then crumbled them back into his pocket.

Chapter 17

Clover rocked back in his chair and rubbed his swollen tummy. "This has been the best week of my life." He looked across the professor's porch at Buddy who, likewise, was sitting in his rocker. He was not rubbing his tummy.

Buddy looked up from reading his paper. "Here comes the professor. I'll be glad when he sits his big head down and blocks you from my view."

"You're not bitter are you, Buddy? I can't help it if I'm a romantic. Louise knows a romantic guy when she sees one."

"You pick a few flowers and now you think you're some decrepit Casanova."

"What kind of creep did you call me?"

"I said decrepit you big…oh, never mind."

"That's what I thought," Clover said with a degree of satisfaction. "It's been five days of homemade heaven. Tonight is barbequed beef with homemade macaroni and cheese. When's the last time Louise cooked for…?" A thought struck Clover, making him stop in mid sentence. "What did you say again?"

"Good evening, professor," Buddy said, doing his best to ignore Clover.

Clover acknowledged the professor with a quick glance and nod and then turned his attention back to Buddy. "Did you say flowers?"

Buddy smirked as he turned his paper to the front page. "I'm sorry. What I meant was Sandhill lilies."

Clover did his best not to appear nervous, but it was obvious when he began stuttering. "Did…did…Lou…Louise tell you that?" Clover just could not believe she would tell. He asked her to keep the lilies a secret. He, of course, did not want to hurt his best friend's feelings. At least that is what he told Louise.

"Oh, no, no," Buddy replied, "I saw a picture of you right here in the…"

"Clover Styron!" And that's about as nice as the words would get. "Do you know how much those lilies are worth?" The voice was female but there was nothing lady-like about it. As Mrs. Jean chewed into Clover with every colorful word in the ol' Beaufort arsenal, Buddy sat back in his chair, jingled his glass of tea and drank with a sense of deep inner peace.

The professor, who any other time would have told the commotion to quiet down, found himself trying to walk quietly up his steps in an effort to not turn the colorful-worded lady's attention. He was not sure if he should hide out in the house or sit on his front porch and enjoy the lively entertainment. He decided to sit and enjoy.

Mrs. Jean stomped up Clover's steps, continuing to showcase her cringing vocabulary, and walloped the terrified man up side his head. It was a blow that made the professor shutter.

Buddy again rattled the ice in his glass and siphoned what was left of his tea. "I'd rather deal with a pack of blistering hemorrhoids than get on that woman's bad side."

"What on earth happened?" the professor asked.

Buddy threw a copy of the *Beaufort Weekly* over to the professor. A large picture of Clover picking lilies from Mrs. Jean's garden covered the front page. The bottom of the page read: Summer brings out the romance in local resident Clover Styron. (Picture courtesy of Buddy Davis)

"Who'd ya give'em to?" Mrs. Jean barked.

"I…I…I…" Clover cowered in his rocker, trying to think of something – anything - to make her stop yelling at him.

"I WANT MY LILLIES BACK."

"I…I…I'll pay you for them."

"They're priceless!" Mrs. Jean continued her screaming.

The loud voices stirred the neighbors from their slumber. Across the street, Louise opened her door and looked around to see where the commotion was coming from.

"Who'd ya give'em to? I'm not going to ask again."

Uncle Frank, stealthy as always, emerged from behind the professor's chair and pointed his finger at Louise. "He gave them to that painted-up woman over there."

Mrs. Jean spun around and eyed Louise. "You little star-let," she whispered before raising her voice to a scream heard up and down Moore street. "I want my lilies back!"

Louise's eyes widened. She walked backwards into her house, locked the door and glanced from behind the curtain. She disappeared for a moment and then returned, again peak-ing from behind the curtain. Once she was sure Mrs. Jean was not too close, she opened the door just wide enough to place a beautiful vase of Sandhill lilies at the foot of the door.

Mrs. Jean marched off Clover's porch and headed straight to Louise's house.

Clover slumped in his chair and placed his hands over his face. "Awe, man." He opened his hands slightly so he could see as Mrs. Jean approached Louise's door. "Awe, man."

Buddy jingled the ice in his tea and then returned to reading his paper. "You oughta enjoy any leftovers you have. Don't suspect we'll be seeing her for a couple of days."

Chapter 18

Angel rolled over and looked at the clock. It was 2:00 am. She typically slept well, but on this evening, she could not seem to clear her mind. It was Jack. She hated that a boy was changing the well-trained pattern of her life. *Why am I thinking about him?* She knew it was just a friendship and she told herself that it could never be anything more than that. He was a young man with so much in front of him. He was only beginning to live and, with her help, slowly leaving behind a life of prejudice and the constant self-inflicted expectation of failure and strife. Jack's personality and well-intended motives were certainly, in Angel's mind, going to deliver him to a more respected and ethical life. He would have the cliché *new life*.

"I'm a handicap," Angel whispered, allowing the deluge of negativity to continue. She was limited in what she could do. She would only hold Jack back. She feared rejection and the possibility of being left behind yet again. First, it was her parents, then her grandmother and eventually, the professor. Then she would be alone in the world. She had been preparing herself for that time since the day she lost her mother and father. An interesting finding in Angel's work (in neuropsychology) was that unless a person actively and consciously controls their thoughts, over 90% of those thoughts will be negative. Essentially, when sin entered the world, the brain began rewiring itself to follow failure and mental suffering, as opposed to happiness and inner peace.

"Stop," Angel said to herself as she sat up in bed. She was disappointed in herself. She knew all to well the necessity of constantly feeding the brain positive affirmations. "I can have anything I set my mind to," she repeated while tapping on her temples. "I can have love in my life. I can take chances without fearing the pain."

Angel removed the covers from her legs and placed a series of electrodes across her thighs and lower legs. Through exercise and electrical stimulation, she had kept her legs from atrophying and, in fact, had actually added some shape to her muscles. This was very rare in a spinal cord injury of her type. Most people continue losing muscle mass and bone strength throughout life until they are no longer able to use their legs at all. Angel was determined not to allow this. By just looking at her and her firm legs, a person could easily mistake her for an athlete and not a spinal cord injury victim.

Angel pushed her chair quietly to the front door and headed out into the dark night. She was not sure exactly where she was going, but found herself drifting toward the church. She thought about Timothy Lee as she moved down Ann Street and did her best to keep her mind from entertaining the thought that he might be out there, watching her and planning who knows what. A cool sea breeze only exacerbated the chill bumps on her arms.

Angel stopped in front of the church. She noticed the flickering of some sort of light from inside that caused a faint glow upon the stained glass. She took a deep breath, hoping it would give her some courage. She then began rolling down the side of the church, heading toward the ancient burying ground.

"This is a first," Angel said aloud after considering the psychosis that one must have to go to an old cemetery, shrouded by even older oak trees whose limbs seemed to stir-up visions of the devils arms.

As Angel rolled along the acorn-covered sidewalk, she peered through the iron fence and into the dark and foggy graveyard.

"That's strange," a voice said from somewhere in the dark, startling Angel. "My ears are vibrating." Jack sat on top of the cannon on Captain Otway Burns' grave.

"Gosh," Angel placed her hand over her chest. "You scared the life out of me."

"That's what happened to a few of the folks in here," Jack said, making a poor attempt at a joke.

"Your ears are vibrating? What does that mean?" Angel asked

"Must be that Law of Attraction thing. You know – the law of sympathetic resonance. It made those piano keys vibrate, so why can't my ears do the same."

"Funny," Angel said with a cynical tone. "You want some company?"

Jack pushed a button to light his watch. "You shouldn't be out this late. There's all kinds of crazies in Beaufort."

"I'm a big girl."

"You're not that big."

"These wheels can move."

"You're crazy," Jack said with a laugh.

"You're the one laying in a graveyard in the middle of the night."

"Just hangin' with the Captain. Having a little heart to heart."

Jack jumped off the cannon and walked over to the gate. He struggled with the lock for a few moments but was unable to reach it from inside the fence. "Meet me at the side door of the church. I'll let you in that way."

Angel wheeled herself to the door, which Jack quickly opened after punching in the security code. Once inside, Angel could see where the flickering light was coming from. At the front of the church, just below the pulpit, sat a table with three candles lit. Beside the table was a pillow, a blanket and a book.

"Camping out?" Angel asked.

Jack appeared embarrassed. "Something like that." He began pushing Angel to the back of the church and through a back door that lead outside to the burying ground.

"What are you reading?"

"It's just a book about renovating historical landmarks. Nothing exciting."

"So you do have passion for something besides graveyards."

"Dead Captains," Jack corrected her.

"Tell me about renovating."

"I could cure your sleeplessness if I did that."

Angel placed her hands on the wheels making the chair come to a stop. "Really, tell me about it."

"It's just something I'm kinda good at. I like the challenge of trying to repair an old building without taking away the beauty of its history. I hate when a renovation looks like, of all things, a renovation."

"Have you done any of that work?" Angel asked.

"Did some of this church, in fact. You can't find this kind of old wood shingle anywhere, so I made them by hand."

"I didn't notice any repairs on it."

"That's the goal."

Jack pushed Angel to Captain Otway's grave. Angel immediately locked the wheels on her chair.

"Can you give me a push up?" she asked.

A tree branch snapped from somewhere behind them and then crashed against the ground. Angel jumped and lost her balance. Before she could fall, Jack caught her by wrapping his arms around her and lifted her back up. Their cheeks brushed each other. Without saying a word, they paused just an inch from each other's lips. Angel blanked her mind and pressed her lips against Jack's. He slid one of his hands up to her shoulder, holding her tighter than before.

"What was that for?" Jack whispered.

"It's for catching me. Don't get any ideas."

Jack smiled but did not speak. Suddenly, he pulled both arms away from Angel and then quickly placed them back before she could fall.

Jack shrugged his shoulders. "Did it again." This time he kissed Angel and made sure the kiss lasted longer than the first.

"Give you an inch and you take a mile," Angel said, unable to conceal her smile.

Jack and Angel sat on top of the cannon, each unable to think of anything to say. *I can't believe I just did that,* Angel thought to herself.

"Let's not let this make things weird," Jack finally broke the silence.

"Let's not," Angel agreed. "Can I ask you a question?"

Jack turned to face Angel. "Certainly."

"You live here, in the church, don't you?"

Jack again appeared embarrassed. "Pathetic isn't it?"

"It's temporary," Angel said with confidence. "One day you'll be a famous old house fixer person."

Jack laughed, "An old house fixer person."

"Can I ask you another question?

"Give you an inch and you take a mile," Jack responded jokingly

"Why did you vandalize this church?"

Jack took a big breath before speaking. "I didn't."

"But, they said you…"

"I was with some friends that night. We had been drinking and they decided to break in."

"So you didn't do it?"

"Guilty by association. I stood outside, but I was here."

"What happened to the others?"

"Nothing."

"Nothing?"

"I took the rap. Nobody knows about them, and they won't."

"Jack, but why?"

"They made a mistake. They're good guys who did something stupid. I tried to talk them out of it, but it didn't help."

"I don't understand why you took all the blame."

"I knew I was going nowhere. They were in college trying to make something of themselves. If they got caught, it would ruin their future."

"But, what about yours?"

"Again, I wasn't going anywhere. I figured if I went to jail, it wouldn't be much different from the life I was living. At least I'd have a place to sleep and eat."

"That's awful," Angel exclaimed.

"That's life."

"That's not life. Where's your family?"

"Mom died of a drug overdose. Dad's in prison on drug charges, of course. Last I heard he was in Morganton."

"Do you ever talk to him?"

"Never have. Never even seen him. Never need to."

"I'm sorry."

"I'm not."

"So, where did you live before?"

"In Greensboro, with my grandmother until she died. Then I was moved here, to Beaufort, to live with foster parents and their son."

"Is he the one who vandalized the church?"

"One of them."

"You just didn't go back?"

"His parents asked me not to. They felt it was best that I didn't hang around their son anymore. You know, bad influence and all."

"So, he gets off scotch clean and you look like the bad guy?"

"It's worth it. He's been a good friend, accepted me like a brother when I first moved here."

"And you never see his parents?"

"No. I'm somewhat of an embarrassment to them, seeing how they helped raise me."

"That's so unfair."

"I don't regret taking the fall."

"And how did you start living in the church?"

"Doug, one of the volunteers who help's maintain the church found me sleeping in the graveyard. He gave me a key and talked to the pastor. Now I work days here and they allow me to stay in the church at night."

"That's awfully nice of them."

"Doug is awesome. He's the closest thing to a father that…" Jack felt a weakness in his voice and paused to gather himself.

Angel smiled and ran her hand across Jack's face. "That's sweet." She then leaned forward and kissed Jack's cheek. "Maybe I should let you get back to your private time with the Captain."

"Will I see you tomorrow?"

"If you're lucky."

"Angel," Jack said as he placed his hand on her elbow, "when do you leave?"

Angel's smile looked more like a frown. "Let's not think about that. Besides, I haven't received any good offers yet. There aren't many schools with a neuropsychology opening." Angel winked at Jack. "Who knows, I just might stay here forever."

"You're right. I shouldn't think about you leaving. I just wanted to know how long to enjoy this. It's been nice having you here."

"That's sweet. But, I think the Captain's getting a little jealous of me taking up your quality time with him."

Jack smiled, "He can be such a stiff."

Chapter 19

The professor arrived early at Front Street. He wanted some time to sit and think. His thoughts, however, were not fully preoccupied with Sharon. He also thought about Beverly. For so many years, he was able to dull the memory of her. But, he always felt the rumble of guilt just below the surface, always waiting for the chance to erupt and overcome him with grief.

"Got something on your mind?" Timothy Lee's voice came from behind the professor.

"I'm surprised you don't know, given your psychic powers."

"There are no psychics, just intuitions."

"And I'm sure you're going to share those intuitions with me."

"I suspect you're thinking about Sharon or Beverly or…"

"Both," the professor chimed in.

"Yes, both. You feel like sharing the story with me?"

"You mean the great Timothy Lee doesn't know the story? You knew about Beverly - somehow."

"I know you must face her story again, soon. And, I know she's a big reason why you hold such animosity toward God."

"There is no God. There simply can't be. And, as for your little verses, they're a pitiful attempt to have science prove the existence of your utopian God."

"I knew you'd do your homework, Professor. Please do share."

"First your little dirt trick. Everything is made out of the same elements because everything came about from the same thing: the Big Bang."

Timothy Lee rubbed his chin. "Interesting, I can see where your faith is."

"It's not faith. It's science."

"Please continue, professor."

"Yes, there are seashells and marine animals on the Earth's mountain peaks…"

"All of them," Timothy Lee interrupted him. "Even the Himalayan Mountains. At the top of those mountains are sea animals that look like crabs. They even have shells. They call them Ammonites."

"And it would seem that these shells and sea animals would point to a major world flood, like Noah's in your Bible."

"I'm really enjoying this, professor. I knew I would."

"I'm surprised someone like you would be so naïve as to forget that shellfish don't move much at all during their entire lives. Maybe inches, but that's it. So, don't you think it's a little silly to think they crawled all the way to Mount Ararat or, as you just pointed out, the Himalaya Mountains, all within a year? Isn't that how long the flood lasted – a year? Those clams would be cruising like a 747."

"Yes, I can see your…"

"Furthermore," the professor interrupted, "do you really believe forty days of rain would cause a flood level high enough to cover the mountain tops of the world? Let's be realistic. I don't mean to sound insulting, but that's so simpleminded. Is it any surprise science can't take this creation argument seriously?"

"Professor, you're right, but also wrong. Read Genesis 7:11. It wasn't just the rain. That would be silly for me to believe. The oceans exploded up, just like those volcano eruptions under the ocean. The power of this sprayed water all over the earth. It was this powerful burst of water that spread marine life to the earth's highest peaks – and deserts."

"Sounds like a good sci-fi movie, but not realistic. Not scientific."

"Professor, on Mount Ararat there's something else strange that's hard to explain. Let me see if I can remember how the Geological Society described it." Timothy Lee broke a stick in half and added it to the pile he had made under his feet. He then picked up the sticks and dropped them all to the ground. They landed, of course, into another haphazard pile. Timothy Lee looked down at the pile and exhaled deeply, seemingly frustrated. "Nothing again," he said as he gathered the sticks and dropped them again. "Another pile. Just another pile of sticks."

The professor remembered his conversations with Buddy and Clover about this habit. Timothy Lee lifted his head suddenly. "Oh, yes. I remember. There are these things called pillow lava, which are the result of hot lava forming under water. The water causes the lava to cool and become a solid. Professor, Mount Ararat is volcanic mountain and they did find pillow lava above the 14,000 foot level. See what that means? The mountain had to be covered by water at some point."

The professor placed his head in his hands in frustration of Timothy Lee's absurd argument. "Look, science knows that the earth was covered by water in its long existence. Everyone knows that. The earth was covered by water and then the continents, along with the mountains, were formed when the earth's plates came together, thus pushing up the mountains and continents we see today. Science proved this a long time ago. You can't blind yourself to the evidence. When you look at both sides and give them a fair shake, it's obvious that evolutionary science holds up. Creation science does not." The professor took a deep breath and rocked back in his chair. "Stop fooling yourself. It's never going to change. Science shows how the earth began and how life began. Science has murdered your God."

"Is that where your faith is, professor?"

"Science is not faith. We've been through this already."

"Faith is something you believe but can't see. Did you see the seashells form when the earth was covered? Did you see the continental shift cause the mountains to form so quickly? You have your evidence, professor, just as I have mine. I have faith in a Creator and you have faith in your science. Either way, it's still faith."

"Timothy, I'm just asking you to be rational. There are layers of fossils across the earth. These form slowly over time, leaving behind the evidence of life during that period."

"That specific period, that specific time in history, correct?" Timothy Lee clarified.

"Yes. These layers are formed one on top of the other, giving us a geographical timeline. When the sea bottoms lifted, they brought the marine life also, which is precisely why you find seashells and sea animals on mountain tops."

"Interesting, Professor. You really did your homework, didn't you?"

"It's really not hard. Look, Timothy, I hope I'm not shattering your faith. You have a right to believe what you want. We can coexist and not agree, right?"

"Of course. Can I ask you another question, professor?"

"Absolutely."

"Humor me, if you would. Let's say I'm right and the waters of the oceans did burst upon the earth. It would leave mass destruction, right?"

"Correct."

"Like a tsunami going through a village, but even worse, yes?"

"Yes."

"And you say these layers are like a timeline, right? For instance, specific creatures should be found in specific layers. Right?"

"I'm not sure where you're going but, yes, that's right."

"So, help me understand why fossils that are from completely different ages are found mixed together? I mean, animals that are thousands of years apart are found mixed together. Not only that, there are trees, and this I find very interesting. There are trees, fossilized, that are found upside-down, right-side up, left angles and right angles. Just a big mess. Like you would expect from a massive, catastrophic tsunami. But, this is the most interesting thing: there are trees that actually pass through numerous fossil layers. These trees look like arrows that were shot through different time periods. So, what does that mean? Certainly, the trees didn't form their top and bottoms thousands of years apart. That would be, as you said before, simpleminded. It tells me something unbelievably destructive happened. Maybe something like a flood, with the oceans exploding across the earth."

The professor looked across the ocean at the afternoon sunset. "Again, I'm quite certain science has an answer for that. Besides, your speculations are not fact. They're wishful thoughts."

"Is that where your faith is, professor?"

"What's with this faith thing?"

"Nothing, it's just something you might need later."

The professor turned away from Timothy Lee and bit his lip. "You mean I might need faith to talk to my wife again? Yes, I might need an awful lot of faith for that."

Timothy Lee looked down the seawall and noticed a figure walking towards him and the professor. "I need to go. About Beverly, I think you might find it helpful to just talk to someone. It helps to get those things out of you. We'll continue our conversation later...tomorrow at sunset?"

The professor sat back in his chair. He thought about what Timothy Lee had said. Maybe he could get it out, the guilt he had kept buried for over forty years. "I'll be here."

Timothy Lee placed a final stick on the pile he had built. He once again picked up the sticks and dropped them to the ground. They landed, as anyone would expect, into another disorganized heap of sticks. Timothy Lee placed both hands on his hips as he looked down at the pile and slowly shook his head. "Thought I had it that time." He gathered the sticks and walked away.

Chapter 20

The professor watched curiously as Timothy Lee left in a hurry. In his previous exits his custom was to walk east, down Front Street, taking a moment to smell the flowers at the entrances of the Cedars and Inlet Inn's. He then looked through the front glass at the Front Street Pharmacy before making his way to Clawson's Restaurant for a sweet bun and a coffee. He was very predictable. But today, he took a different route, almost as if he was trying to avoid the person walking towards them.

The professor's curiosity got the best of him, so he tried following behind Timothy Lee, who quickly crossed to the other side of Front Street and made his way across to the back-side of Ann Street. Timothy Lee was always efficient at leaving, and this would be no different from his previous exits.

The professor looked up and down Ann Street, with no sight of the madman. Seeing no use in trying to search any farther, he made his way back to the sitting spot, planning to spend the remaining twilight watching the wild horses grazing on Carrot Island and the sun sinking like a great ship into the slumbering ocean. However, when he lifted his head to look for cars along Front Street that he noticed another person sitting in one of the rockers.

"Michael," the voice sounded before the professor could turn away. "Chance Gordon. We met the other night."

The professor nodded and, like a sulking child, walked across the street and sat down beside the young man.

"Looks like we share the same quiet place," Chance said.

"Looks that way," the professor agreed.

"You doing okay, Mike?"

The professor nodded his head. "I'm hanging in there."

"That man you were talking to just now, who was that?"

"It's nobody you want to know."

Chance accepted the professor's reply. "Are these your chairs?"

"No." The professor's voice was not congenial, nor was it altogether belligerent. It was indifferent.

Chance smiled warmly at the professor before leaning back in the chair and taking a moment to admire its smooth finish. "I liked the old ones better, to be honest."

"To be honest...," the professor repeated before trailing off. "What else would you be?"

Chance smiled again. "Dishonest."

The professor chuckled.

"Ah-ha, I knew I could make you laugh eventually."

"Aren't you a pastor?"

"I am, indeed."

"So, shouldn't it be some sort of an endeavor on your part to tell the truth?"

A look of confusion replaced the smile on Chance's face. "Okay, where exactly did I miss the turn here? Weren't you just laughing?"

"I chortled."

"You, who?" asked Chance.

The professor smiled. "Pastor's should tell the truth, yet you just told me a lie."

Chance rubbed his forehead with the palm of his hand.

"You said that you knew you could make me laugh. Were you telling the truth? Did you really think so?"

This time Chance chuckled in disbelief. "You're serious, aren't you?"

"I am."

"It was just a statement...or, a phrase...or a..." Chance struggled to find the right description of such an innocent...

"Lie," the professor said with a snigger.

Chance stared at the professor, completely bewildered. "You just laughed."

The professor rocked back in his chair and smiled. "I chortled."

"Chortled," Chance said to himself, still shaking his head. "Where'd you learn that word?"

"You're bamboozled, aren't you?" the professor asked, now with a broad smile across his face.

"I give up," Chance said as he picked up a stick that was lying beneath the rocking chair. He dropped it on the ground and picked it up again. "You want to see something really funny?"

Chance pointed in the direction of a heavy man in a uniform walking gingerly through the shells, making his way to the creek. The man pointed at a group of people fishing nearby and gave them the 'stop signal' with his hand. He then pulled out a test tube and filled it with water.

"What's so funny about that?" the professor asked. "He's just testing the water. It's called the Marine Patrol. Didn't you say you grew up here?"

The professor had a jaded look on his face as he turned away from Chance and looked again at the large man. The man lifted the tube up with his right hand and swirled it around. He examined it closely against the fading sun. He used his left hand to hold up his sagging pants.

"That is kind of funny," the professor admitted.

"Kind of," Chance agreed.

The large man whiffed the tube under his nose and then emptied it into his mouth.

"Did he just drink that filthy water?" the professor asked, his voice low and concerned.

The man swished the water around in his mouth.

"No."

The professor winced.

The man spit the water out.

The professor winced again. "What on earth?"

The man looked over at the group of people and gave them the thumbs-up. "You're good to go," he said with a look of satisfaction.

"Who is that?" the professor asked, partly impressed but mostly disgusted.

"That man is famous around here. He saved my life one time. Drug me out of the river during a hurricane."

The professor looked up at Chance. He held tight to his sophisticated demeanor. "So, he did."

"He did, indeed," Chance said, with admiration, as the man stumbled back through the shells and made his way to solid ground. "But, that's a long story." Chance looked out across Taylor's Creek one last time before holding his hand out. The professor stood to shake it.

"I hope I didn't irritate you too much, Chance."

Chanced waved. "Not at all. Maybe a little bamboozled, but not irritated."

The professor smiled.

"Gotta catch my ride. The Diesel's waiting."

"I never caught your friend's name," the professor said as Chance jogged away.

"I just told you."

"No…"

"Yes, I did," Chance cut the professor off.

The professor placed his hand over his mouth and lowered his right brow. He found himself at a loss by Chance's answer.

"His name is Diesel."

Chapter 21

After Chance left with Diesel, the professor sat back in his rocking chair and waited for nightfall and its company of stars. It became quite windy as the ocean breezes meandered over and through the dense brush of Carrot Island before racing across the pitch-black creek, freely skimming the small waves until they finely brushed across the professor's face.

"Got something on your mind, professor?"

The professor did not turn his head. He now recognized the voice well. "There's always something on my mind. What brings you back?"

"You."

"Can't get enough of me, can you?"

"I'm worried about you. I want you to come to terms with your past."

"Can you just let it go? It's my past, not yours or anybody else's."

"The truth may not be altogether nice, but it's much better than what her family believes to be true. There are usually two sides to every story. Those that hold animosity toward you should know your side. They should know the truth."

"The truth doesn't matter anymore. I destroyed her life. I've paid the price for what I did and I'm still paying it."

"Your past is closer to you than you think. It's coming back. It's time to get ready for it, to get the story straight. You're not a bad person, professor. Love chose you. You didn't choose it."

The professor turned around to face the stranger, but when he did, there was no one there. The wind blew harder, causing the chairs to sway and the sound of chimes to ring out from somewhere in the darkness. Chills ran up the professor's spine and his body became still and weak. Even if he wanted to run, he could not.

"I know I'm not crazy," the professor said to himself, barely audible.

"Why would you think you're crazy, professor?" Timothy Lee stood a few yards away, just outside of the field of vision.

The professor whirled around to see where the voice was coming from. Timothy Lee stood at ease in the wind. The professor said nothing and instead just studied the man. He was a fairly young man, no older than forty-five. His curly brown hair was well trained -- not a single strand out of place. His face was smooth with freshly shaved cheeks that show-cased eyes of piercing, deep green. His expression was alluring and, yet, tranquil. A persistent smile dominated the right side of the stranger's mouth and a faint sparkle made its home in the right eye, as well. Even his impeccably trimmed eyebrows were cared for with the utmost attention.

"You look like you've seen a ghost, professor."

"I…I thought you were behind me," he said with a stutter.

Timothy Lee smiled and walked down to the shoreline to admire the stars. "Professor, do you believe in life after death."

The professor made no comment as the sharp chill of nerves ran up his back, causing the fine hairs upon his neck to stand on end. He was not surprised the mind could make hairs do this without even being touched. Angel had enlightened him to this phenomenon on occasion. She used it as one of her demonstrations of the power of thought.

"I can prove it to you."

The professor said nothing.

"God has put clues all around us. In fact, right now you are looking at life after death."

The professor felt another round of chills running down his spine. *Surely this man isn't suggesting that he's a spirit.*

Timothy Lee turned and faced the professor. "Look above, at the night sky. It's there that you will see it. It's there that you will see life after death."

The professor was confused and wondered if perhaps the stranger was suffering from another level of mania.

"Would you agree that we are, from a purely scientific standpoint, made up of energy?" Before the professor could answer, not that he even planned to, Timothy Lee spoke further. "This never sank in with me until I learned about medical tests such as EKG's, EEG's and MRI's. The EKG measures energy from the heart while the EEG measures energy from the brain. And the one that really got me thinking was the MRI. This machine has a big magnet that flips ions in the body and then, as you have already guessed, takes pictures of the energy given off from these. You can see an actual picture of the body's insides!"

The professor followed the stranger's analogies, but found them unimpressive and mostly commonsensical.

"It's the stars, professor. Their light is beautiful. Yet those stars are dead. Been dead for who knows how long. Science says many millions of years or more. But, we can still see their starlight. Their light continues to travel through space, forever. That's life after death." Timothy Lee turned around and faced the professor. "Stars live forever. Even when they are dead, we can still see their light, their photons, and their energy. Science has taught you that energy can be *neither* created nor *destroyed*. Therefore, I argue that neither can we be created by chance or destroyed by death." Timothy Lee sensed the professor's hesitance. "Look, if you don't buy anything else I've said tonight, just remember, those beautiful stars are dead and yet they live on forever."

Nothing else was said between the two men until Timothy Lee picked up his pile of sticks and turned to leave. "Even the light from the fires you built in your Oxford room still lives on. Though you thought you buried them, they still live and will soon turn full circle on you."

The professor's heart dropped. *How could he know?*

"Goodnight, professor. I'll see you tomorrow."

University of Oxford, England
Forty-four years earlier...

Michael Valentine wondered how he would make it a year away from the woman he had asked, just a few weeks before, to marry him. Being at Oxford was the opportunity of a lifetime. Surely, he could not turn around and run home because he was lovesick and lonely. He wanted to be adventurous and brave. That's the way he wanted Beverly to remember him while he was away. Yet, he could not help but stand quiet, alone, and think of her back home, living out her senior year without him. He was her first of many things, including her first boyfriend. She never trusted boys growing up, a product of living in a house where her father was consistent in only one thing: extra-marital affairs. Michael was determined to make her trust him. But, now he was an ocean away and she was alone with her sorority sisters. Maybe she was the one being adventurous.

Michael ran his fingers across the rough stone encasement that made up the old wood-burning fireplace in his dormitory. Never would you find a stone fireplace, or any kind of fireplace for that matter, in an American dorm, he thought. It was an ancient fireplace. Certainly not as old as the castle-like towers that had welcomed students of the Magdalen College branch of Oxford since 1448, but nonetheless, old. Michael wondered how many souls had stood in his footsteps, running their fingers across that same surface. Countless, he could only imagine. The building was called the "New Building." However, there was nothing new about it, except when one considered that Oxford was founded in the 12th century.

Certainly, the New Building had undergone its share of face-lifts, but every effort was made to keep it looking as it would have a half millennium before. Many of the same roads still existed, their large cobblestone potholes being strong evidence of this fact. The campus itself reminded one of a grand Irish castle, rather than a place of higher education. Michael could feel the humbling chill of history in the rooms.

A thick hearthrug lay in front of the fireplace while candle-bearing sconces hung from the walls to supply any additional light-ing needed, especially on a cold, moonless night. The hallways were long and dimly lit, with cold granite floors except where there were long, well-kept rugs. It was altogether lovely and nostalgic. It would have been near perfect, if only Beverly were standing beside him.

The brief knock at the door was more to warn that someone was coming in, whether invited or not. When Michael helped complete the task of opening the door, he met eyes with a very curious and, even more so, beautiful young lady.

"How did you get it?" she asked as she walked past Michael and spun in circles, admiring the room as if it were some Narnian wonderland. And, in a way, it was.

"Get what?" Michael asked, completely unaware of anything he had gained on this trip besides a heavy heart.

The young lady paused her purling admiration of the surroundings long enough to give Michael a punch on the arm. "Get out!"

Michael took her literally. "But this is my room…" Before he finished his plea, the girl again punched him on the arm.

"I can't believe they actually gave this room to an American student."

Michael decided it was best to avoid any further confrontation. This was England, after all, and he felt obligated to respect the tradition of English gentlemen. Then again, Michael could not say that he knew any Englishmen. Nor could he say that he knew any gentlemen, period.

"Is there something special about this room?" he asked.

"You really don't know?"

"I really don't know," Michael repeated.

"Surely you know who C.S. Lewis is?"

"The Narnia books?"

"And many others."

"C.S. Lewis lived here?"

"Not only that, he wrote some of his books here and shared them with his friend; a guy by the name of J.R.R. Tolkein."

"The Hobbit."

"The Hobbit," the excited girl repeated, before walking over to the fireplace. "C.S. Lewis would come home each night, make a fire and settle in with a cup of hot tea and whatever book he was reading."

Michael returned to the fireplace and ran his finger across the top of its stone borders. "A fire and a book. That sounds like a good way to end a day."

"Do you know how to start a fire?" the girl asked, still giddy about her presence in the famed C.S. Lewis Oxford dormitory, a place where some of histories greatest apologetics were written in front of the same fireplace she now faced.

"I believe I can," Michael said without much thought.

The young lady held out her hand. "I'm Sharon."

Chapter 22

Damage control. That was the only thing on Clover's mind since the lily catastrophe with Ms. Jean. Louise, embarrassed to the point of a self-imposed house confinement, was spending her time inside with curtains closed. She was mourning the death of her hard earned, dignified reputation. Clover noticed Buddy was not around much during dinnertime. He knew the reality, the cold, hard truth of his predicament.

Clover sat fully clothed on his toilet with his head slumped downward. This was his sacred place when he needed to think or meditate on a problem at hand. Regardless of whether he really needed to use the facility, he sat, sometimes for hours, and thought. He brought in food, drinks and books; sometimes even a portable radio so he could sing along with teary-eyed country songs. He discovered many very important facts in the john when he was thinking. Recently he learned why it's called a "john" to begin with. The answer, Clover proudly revealed to the misfortunate folks sitting at his table during the Wednesday Night church dinner, was because a man by the name of John Harington built the first indoor bathroom, or water closet, as it was called then, for Queen Elizabeth I. Thus, folks began calling the bathroom the "john." Clover decided to call his the "Johnny," which he felt honored the great

John Harington while at the same time giving it an American flavor.

It was during an old George Jones song that the idea came to him. He figured that there were two options for Louise, either himself or Buddy. As far as he could tell, there were no other contestants competing for her hand – the hand that could cook anything from scrumptious macaroni and cheese to fried okra. He loved those beautiful hands. Clover shook his head, trying to get the images of food to subside. He then recalled his father once saying, in his wisdom, that when two friends came across a bear in the woods, survival came down to this: you did not necessarily have to outrun the bear; you only needed to outrun your friend. Clover, still remembered as the gray squirrel, was ready to outrun Buddy for good.

Angel opened the letter slowly. She was nervous; nervous that the University of Chicago, the school she dreamed of attending since discovering her love for neuropsychology, would not accept her as a graduate student teacher. She was also nervous that they would.

She read the letter, placed it on her bed, and then cried.

Chapter 23

Timothy Lee looked up and down Front Street before straightening his wig and quickly disappearing behind the corner store. Pharmacy break-ins were by no means an uncommon event in big-town America, but in small-town Beaufort, it had never happened. Things were about to change.

The lock posed no real obstacle for Timothy Lee's skilled hands. Once inside, he wasted no time finding the medications he simply could not live without. The Percocet came first. He emptied the three bottles into a bag and then placed the empty containers back to their rightful positions on the shelf. He then slid a crowbar from under his jacket and proceeded to break the lock that protected the most important drug. The OxyContin felt delightful sliding down his throat, but not nearly as delightful as when it began stimulating the "feel good" receptors in his brain. Timothy Lee crushed an additional tablet in his mouth before sitting down and awaiting the welcomed euphoria. He then placed the remaining tablets in another bag and with stealth-like efficiency made his way to the end of Front Street, where he found the two white, pristine rocking chairs. As the cool north winds pushed back the sticky summer heat, he felt the rush of his drugs quickly filtering out all the pain of his world. His eyes rolled back and he fell into a peaceful stupor.

A few hours had passed when Timothy Lee was awakened by a firm grip on his shoulder.

"Sir, I need you to put your hands in the air. I need to see both of them. And do it slowly. Understand?" The police officer towered over Timothy Lee, his free hand strategically placed on the strap above his gun.

Timothy Lee kept his face down as he slowly stood. He was only half way up when the officer aggressively forced him back down into his chair. Timothy Lee released his grip on the drugs in his pocket and slowly raised his arms being careful not to shift his wig.

"I'm not armed officer. I'm no criminal, I assure you."

"I need you to stand with your arms above your head." Timothy Lee slowly rose to his feet and followed the officer's instructions.

"Turn around and place your hands behind your back."

"Yes sir, officer," Timothy Lee said with a respectful tone.

It was when the officer reached for his cuffs that Timothy Lee did what he knew he had to do. As swift as a cat, he swung around and buried his long, gritty fingernails into the officer's eyes. The feeling of his nails scraping across the moist tissue of the officer's eyes was almost as euphoric as his OxyContin induced ecstasy.

The officer screamed out as he fell to the ground in pain, his hands covering his wounded eyes. Timothy Lee, still feeling high from the drugs, gave the officer a well-aimed kick to the ribs causing him to groan and roll face down in an attempt to protect himself.

Timothy Lee then took a moment to enjoy his work before disappearing into the night.

Chapter 24

Jack sat at the base of Captain Otway Burn's grave and tossed acorns across the dirt path that separated the lots. The afternoon was hot and sticky, but the densely shaded graveyard remained cool and unaffected by the humidity. Angel had been gone the last two days visiting the University of Chicago's Neuropsychology department. She would learn her fate soon. Jack expected the worse. He always expected the worse, mostly because life always gave him the worse. Therefore, at that moment, his heart felt anxious, almost trembling like a hand would when nervous. His mind felt guilt, guilt that he wished she would not like the school, guilt for his wishes, selfish as they were, that she would stay in Beaufort with him, forever. But, Jack knew better. He knew that Angel had bigger dreams and a bigger future than what Beaufort could provide her. Moreover, she definitely had a bigger future than spending her life with a homeless ex-con who spent time in a graveyard, talking to a sea captain who had been dead for almost 200 years. Besides the obvious reasons she could not stay, she also loved her work and needed to follow whatever path it laid down, even if that path took her far away from Beaufort and far away from him.

"Where's the lady friend?" Doug asked as he propped himself against a grave opposite Jack.

"She's out of town for a few days visiting a school in Chicago." Jack kept his head down, not wanting Doug to see his long face and irritated eyes. "The school sent her a letter last week to tell her that she's one of the finalists for acceptance there. That's where she's always wanted to go."

"Chicago's a nice place. I've been there once." Doug nodded his head as if to verify to himself what he was saying. "Yep, nice. But, no Beaufort. Give me Beaufort any day."

Jack looked at Doug with a sheepish smile. "Yeah, where else can a homeless, convicted criminal find a nice graveyard to hang out in?"

"I used to do this tour, you know. Pretty good at it in fact. I used to add my own stuff to it. Things like last words spoken by famous people."

"That sounds very uplifting," Jack said, somewhat jestingly.

"It can be uplifting. John Quincy Adams said, 'This is the last day of earth! I am content'. Evangelist Henry Ward Beecheer said, 'Now comes the mystery'. Shall I continue?"

"Don't let me stop you." Jack always enjoyed Doug's company, though he did not always admit it.

Doug flexed his head and thought for a minute. "Here's a good one: Beethoven said, 'Friends applaud, the comedy is finished'. Humphrey Bogart: 'I should never have switched from Scotch to Martinis'. The writer Elizabeth Barrett Browning answered her husband when he asked her how she felt, 'Beautiful'."

"You ever read any of her stories, Doug?" Jack asked the question feeling it would be a rhetorical 'no'.

"Just quoted her, didn't I?"

"Of course you did."

"Here's a writer I have read. Ever heard of Lord Byron? Before he took his last breath he said, 'Now I shall go to sleep. Goodnight'. Winston Churchill's last words: 'I'm bored with it all'."

Jack laughed at Doug's ability to remember such trivia. "How many times did you give that talk?" he asked, referring to the graveyard tour.

"Hundreds and still going," Doug answered. "Bing Crosby said, 'That was a great game of golf, fellars'. Thomas Edison whispered, 'It is very beautiful over there'." Doug reached forward and placed his hand on Jack's shoe. "And my favorite: Queen Elizabeth I whispered, 'All my possessions for a moment of time'." Doug let the quote soak in for a minute. "Don't waste your time. You've got to get out of this graveyard."

Jack nodded his head. "Don't think so, Doug. This is the only thing I do well."

"Son, you have more to offer this world than you will ever need. You're a good kid. I don't know why you did the things you did to this church, but I have faith in you. And, again I'll say it – anytime you're ready, you don't even need to ask, just come on over to the house and sit down for dinner. You can stay as long as you want. We have an extra room upstairs."

Jack kept his head down.

"Anytime. You understand?" Doug repeated.

"I'm okay here, Doug." Jack's face was not pleasant, instead distorted with a pain Doug had not seen before. Jack, by nature, was chronically jovial and rarely without a smile upon his face.

"Missing your Grandma," Doug said, more of a statement than a question.

"Missing my Grandma," Jack repeated.

Doug knew there was nothing to say. His grandmother raised him and showered him with love. But, even to her, life had been unkind. She had a disability that controlled her life and seemed to curse everything in it. She was married twice and both times her husband left a note on the gas stove saying goodbye. She sobbed when her first husband left. She hardly cried when the second left. She expected it. Her daughter, Jack's mother, watched the way men treated her mother and therefore fell into the same trap. Her husband, who was Jack's true father, beat her, sold drugs and went to prison for combining those two vices on another woman. Jack's mother later made her bed in prison for selling and consuming drugs of her own. Once released, she rekindled her love of drugs and died after overdosing on heroin.

Jack's grandmother blamed herself for her daughter's chosen path in life. And, it was with this guilt that she also passed away. Jack, of course, was lost without her.

Doug moved his jaw from side to side and creased his brows, lost for a moment in thought. He then placed his thumb and index finger across his mouth, looked Jack in the eyes and tossed a pair of keys to him.

"What's this for?" Jack asked as he examined the keys.

"It's not much," Doug replied. "Found it over at Laughton's Garage. Just thought you would need it with your new job."

"New job? Are you firing me?"

"Presbyterian church called asking who was doing our remodeling. Said they loved the work and wanted to make some improvements over there. Gonna pay you pretty good, too."

Jack could not hide his smile. Somebody actually *needed* him. He had become so used to needing others that he forgot the feeling of someone needing him.

"It's a truck," Doug said, enticing a slightly broader grin from Jack.

When Jack walked around the corner of the church, he saw a small pick-up truck parked against the sidewalk. On the side door of the truck was a magnet sign that read: *Jack's Historical Restorations.* Jack stopped and stood silent. It was his own business, a chance to do something with his life.

Doug patted Jack on the back. "Had Rodney Fulcher's law firm set up your own business. You're a legal entity now. Pastor Ann and Pastor Eric are using the Pastor's Discretionary Fund to get you a yellow page ad and some ads in the paper. I don't suspect you're be needing any advertising. You've got a God-given gift, son. Word of mouth is going to keep you busy."

Fighting back the urge to cry, Jack opened his mouth to thank Doug, but the words became lost in a babble of incoherent attempts to speak. "I can't believe this," Jack said. "I can't believe I have my own business. I can't believe I have my own truck."

"I just feel sorry for the pedestrians," Doug chimed in. "We'll get your license tomorrow." Doug looked up at the late afternoon sky. "What do you say we go for a little walk?"

Jack's heart filled with joy. He could not wait to tell Angel about it all. "Sure you don't want me to drive?"

Doug breathed deeply and said, "I'm sure."

The stores along Front Street were bustling with activity. Large boats lined the Beaufort Dock as the ship hands busied themselves with cleaning the decks. It looked like a promising tourist season, which was a welcomed sign for the seasonal businesses. Without tourism, there really was no other significant source of income for the storeowners.

"So, your girlfriend flew off to Chicago." Doug walked with his hands in his pockets and his head looking down at the ground, taking any opportunity he had to kick pebbles along the sidewalk.

"Yup."

Doug waited for Jack to open up and elaborate on the situation with Angel. Jack made no further replies.

"Anybody ever tell you that you are a wonderful conversationalist?"

"Nope."

"There's a reason for that, you know."

"Probably is."

As Doug and Jack walked along Taylor's Creek, they noticed a man breaking a thick branch over his knee. He then took a moment to study the splintered stick before tossing it into the water. When they got closer, the man turned to them and smiled.

"Hasn't rained in two weeks," the stranger said as he watched the stick quickly resurface and bob up and down. "It's hard to sink anything with the salt so thick."

Doug and Jack made no replies to the stranger, although both did consider the fact that it had not rained in some time. This would certainly make the water more salty. Why the stranger thought that should be important to them, they did not know. Jack thought that maybe the man was simply friendly. His appearance seemed friendly enough. He was a fairly young man, no older than forty-five. His curly brown hair was well trained - not a single strand out of place. His face was smooth with freshly shaved cheeks that showcased eyes of piercing, deep green. His expression was alluring and, yet, tranquil. A persistent smile dominated the right side of the stranger's mouth and a faint sparkle made its home in the right eye, as well. Even his impeccably trimmed eyebrows were cared for with the utmost attention. The man was, all things considered, strangely…pleasant.

After Doug and Jack moved on, Timothy Lee walked a short distance to the shiny white rocking chairs and made himself comfortable. He leaned his head back, inhaled deeply, as if savoring the smell of salty air for the first time in a long while, and smiled.

Chapter 25

Clover was having a bad day. He did not sleep particularly well, his mind preoccupied with Louise, of course, and was therefore in a morning stupor when he mistakenly used hemorrhoid cream instead of toothpaste on his toothbrush. His upper lip cringed immediately, bringing half of his distorted face with it.

Things did not get much better during Clover's weekly visit to the park. The park, for many people, is a place to play with children or grandchildren, and maybe even toss a Frisbee for the pooch. Clover recognized the potential in such recreational venues. There were grandmothers spotted at such places, many of them single or widowed, and experienced bakers, roasters and fryers.

Going to the park without a kid or a dog was too obvious, even for a person of Clover's desperation, to risk. So, it took some extra time on the "Johnny" but the answer, as always, became clear to Clover before his finished his sandwich and whatever other inappropriate combination of events he corralled while sitting there.

The dog's name was Maggie, a beautiful mix of lab and poodle, known as a lab-a-doodle. Her owner's were a young couple down the street, whom Clover had never spoken to before. The couple was therefore confused and concerned when he knocked on their front door with a strange request.

"Can I borrow your dog?"

The young man looked back at his wife, wondering if perhaps she knew the man at the door.

"I'll bring her back." Clover lacked social skills in many different areas. "I'm in a hurry if you don't mind."

Brian, the young man standing in front of Clover, found the determination in Clover's eyes unnerving. "Sir, I'm not sure I know you."

"I'm Clover." He looked down at his watch. "Really am in a hurry. So, can I borrow your dog?"

"No." The door shut quickly.

After Clover kidnapped Maggie from the back yard, he walked her briskly to the park and then scoped out the possibilities. Maybe it was the polished shine of the slide but for whatever reason, he focused on a lady with what he assumed was her granddaughter. The young child pointed excitedly to the slide and became progressively distraught as her grandmother nodded "no." Clover, like a predator sensing weakness in a prey, pounced over to the lady, dragging Maggie who was bucking behind like a wild horse. Halfway there Clover stopped and pulled his shorts a little higher to the bottom of his chest. He, if no one else, admired his legs and did his best to reveal them as much as possible. Clover's fashion repulsed Buddy, most notably his insistence on wearing floppy socks. "You look like a rooster wearing socks," he often said.

"It's a hot one," Clover said before introducing himself and *his* dog.

"It is humid," the woman replied, taking care not to offer her name.

Clover introduced himself again, this time smiling and exposing his pearly not so white, more-so-yellowish-brown teeth. "So, do you believe in love at first sight, or should I walk by again?"

The lady backed farther away. Clover turned his attention to the little girl.

"I bet somebody wants to slide down that slide."

The little girl hid her face into her grandmother's side.

"Ah, come on. It'll be fun. These old slides are the best. Much better than those covered plastic slides."

The little girl did not answer. Her grandmother pulled her back another foot.

"It's not scary. It's fun. I tell you what, I'll do it first."

Clover climbed the steps of the slide and took a moment at the top to wave to the little girl. Maggie, the kidnapped dog, had considered running, but evidently decided to stick around as the strange man maneuvered into position on the slide. It began surprisingly gracefully, but only up until the point that Clover sat down on the sun-cooked slide. When his upper thighs made contact with the molten hot steel, he let out a scream that caused the entire playground to pause and take note of what was going on. When he lifted his legs off the slide, his fabric pants allowed his body weight to speed down the slide until the skin on his legs once again grabbed the hot surface. The little girl thought the sound of fingernails down a chalkboard was a hideous sound, but even that had no comparison to the sound of Clover's skin peeling to a stop halfway down the slide. The grandmother closed the little girl's ears as Clover screamed out a string of inappropriate words. She then grabbed the little girl's hand and walked, quite deliberately, away.

Clover pulled his pants up higher in an effort to keep the fabric from rubbing his burnt skin. "I think I've got third degree burns," Clover said as he walked gingerly and bowlegged away from the slide. "Dang thing must be a thousand degrees. What kind of idiot designs a metal slide? You can cook eggs on that thing."

Clover continued his careful gait to the dog. When he passed another woman with her young child on a swing, he momentarily forgot about the burns on his legs. "How you doing, darling?" he asked, still holding his pants up.

The woman looked away in disgust.

"You know, if I received a nickel every time I saw a woman as beautiful as you, I'd have a nickel."

"Please go away."

The woman's comment did not affect Clover at all. After all, he had heard worse on many occasions.

"I may not be the most handsome man here, but I'm the only one talking to you. You're too old anyway. I prefer someone whose skin fits a little better."

As Clover walked farther to grab Maggie, he heard the streaking sounds of police sirens get closer until they pulled into the park. When he saw Maggie's owners step out of the car with two officers, he made a rash decision. *I'm old he thought. Too old to go to jail and share a room with a murderer or rapist.* So Clover did something that only the infamous Gray Squirrel would do. He dropped the leash and ran.

Every few strides Clover hollered out in pain as his shorts rubbed against his burnt legs causing him to skip for a step or two. The first obstacle was a small child. Clover hurdled him with no problem. It was the second obstacle that proved more difficult. The old fence surrounding the park was a five-footer – just tall enough for Clover to second-guess his ability to clear it. He grabbed the top pole with both hands and tried to throw himself over. But, when his pants snagged on a fence wire, he found himself hanging upside down with his denims strapped securely around his ankles. The face of a police officer appeared above him, shaking her head.

Clover looked up at the officer. "Good afternoon Officer. Is there a problem?"

Chapter 26

Jack was just finishing a late afternoon tour when he noticed Angel sitting quietly at the back of the group.

"Are there any ghosts in the graveyard?" a little girl asked.

"Well, I usually don't let this secret out but I can say this. Occasionally at night, people swear they have seen a girl sitting on top of Captain Otway Burns' cannon. They say this girl is the most beautiful creature they have ever seen. In fact, they say mere human words cannot begin to describe her radiance and her natural beauty."

The little girl grabbed her father's arm for protection. "Have you ever seen her?"

Jack puts on his scariest face. "Not only have I seen her, I've kissed her."

"Yuck. You shouldn't kiss ghosts."

"No, no, little one. I didn't kiss a ghost, I kissed an angel."

Angel rolled her eyes and made a gagging gesture with her finger.

After the group dispersed, Jack walked up to Angel and gave her a kiss on the forehead. She returned the weak gesture by grabbing Jack's ears and kissing him on the lips.

"I take it you missed me?"

"Not really," Angel replied slyly. "Okay, maybe just a little bit."

"You missed me. I can tell. So, how was it? Everything you dreamed of?"

Angel hunched her shoulders. "It was just okay. It's crazy, I know, but I kind of missed…"

"Me," Jack interrupted.

"Actually, no. I missed Captain Otway."

"So my competition is a dead man. That really does a lot for my ego."

"I'm just kidding silly. Of course, I missed you."

"Ha, I knew it!" Jack said loudly.

"Don't get a big head now."

"Check these out." Jack pulled out the keys to his new truck and twirled them around his finger.

"You bought a car?"

"A truck actually. My *business* truck. Doug got it for me."

"A business truck. What business are you talking about?"

Jack's smile broadened. "You're looking at the new owner of *Jack's Historical Renovations*. Start my first job Monday."

"That's great news." Angel reached up and slapped Jack on the shoulder. "You see what begins to happen when you take control of your thoughts?"

"Maybe, I'm still not sold that I'll make it yet."

"Of course you'll make it. I'm gonna kick you in the butt until you do."

"But you're leaving soon. You can't kick me in the butt from Chicago."

"Nobody said for sure that I was going to Chicago." Angel grabbed Jack's hand and winked at him. "I really did miss you."

Jack smiled. "I really missed you, too."

Chapter 27

On a summer's night in Beaufort, you can hear the most wonderful recipe of crying seagulls, chirping crickets and weary boat engines fighting their way through the tide. Add to that the starlit night sky and the blinking fireflies and you have the most beautiful place on earth.

The professor sat alone, thinking back to the days he deceived the first love of his life:

University of Oxford, England
Forty-four years earlier...

"I miss you too, Darling," Michael said as he put the finishing touches on his hair. He wanted to look just right.

"Michael," Beverly's voice came through the telephone, "I was thinking of flying out to see you. We could backpack across Europe together."

Michael placed his brush down slowly. His words stumbled at first: "Well, that sounds wonderful. It really does."

"I thought it would help my homesick little puppy. I'll fly out next week then."

"Beverly, I'm…I'm just not so sure you would enjoy it with me being in classes and all the other activities I have to do. Maybe," he took a deep breathe before diving in, "Maybe you shouldn't this semester. Maybe we could come back together next year. Then I'll know my way around a little better. Wouldn't it be romantic? Just the two of us with nothing else to do. I was thinking maybe it would be a nice honeymoon."

Michael felt guilty, but continuingly told himself that he was not doing anything wrong. He really did want to come back with Beverly alone. Certainly they would enjoy it more then. Wouldn't they? Besides, he really wasn't doing anything wrong. Sure, he liked Sharon's spunkiness and wit. He admittedly looked forward to seeing her each day. And, maybe he did feel a little jealous when she talked to the English guys. But, it was just an innocent and temporary curiosity in an intriguing person. Michael was convinced that Sharon was just a familiar person in an unfamiliar place. He was engaged to the woman of his dreams, his one true love. Sharon could never harm his relationship with Beverly. He kept telling himself this. And he was almost convinced of that, almost.

Beverly felt hurt and rejected at first. However, after thinking it through, she realized that maybe Michael was right. Besides, it would be wonderfully romantic to trek across Europe together for their honeymoon.

"I understand. But promise me that we will definitely go there for the honeymoon."

Michael closed his eyes tight and filled his lungs before he answered, "I promise."

Chapter 28

"Am I interrupting something?"

Timothy Lee's sudden appearance did not startle the professor. He had grown quite use to it. "Of course," he answered without looking up.

"Lost in the past?"

"Is there anything wrong with that?"

"Oh, heaven's no. There is nothing wrong with reflecting on the past or even visiting the past. I do it myself. It's an essence of life. We live chapter after chapter, some good, some not so good."

"You bringing my past back adds to my growing list of bad ones."

"No, Professor. You brought back the past. I'm just here to help you through it."

"I didn't ask for your help."

"I wasn't commissioned by you."

The professor finally looked up at Timothy Lee. His eyes were red and angry. "It's not a good time for this."

"Then why are you here, professor? In this spot where you know I will be?" Timothy Lee asked.

The professor's frustration had reached its limit. "Enough with your parables. You're just another fraud. Picking up little tidbits of information, just enough to make it seem like you know something you really do not. You've brought up a bunch of questions, but no answers. I haven't seen my wife, nor will I." The professor walked up to Timothy Lee's face. His lip snarled and his teeth clinched. "If there really is a devil, I think it might be you."

"Please, professor. I know what I say seems to fill you with pain. But this is not pain. It's healing. You cannot understand the ways of the Lord."

"The Lord? The same Lord that my wife prayed to? Look where that got her. Doesn't *your* Lord say that if you ask you will receive?"

"It's not that simple," Timothy Lee began before the professor abruptly cut him off.

"If there is a Lord, he lied," the professor said before lifting one of the rocking chairs and crushing it into the ground. Pieces of wood shattered in all directions, one coming to rest just in front of Timothy Lee's foot.

"You shouldn't have done that, professor. That chair was not yours."

The professor placed his hands on his knees and stared down at the hard ground. "I'll buy you a new one."

"They're not mine," Timothy Lee replied as he gathered up a few pieces of the chair and then dropped them to the ground. "Her prayers really were answered, professor. She prayed earnestly and God gave her what he has promised those who pray with all their heart."

"She died. She didn't pray to die. She wanted to live." The professor's voice fell weak. "She wanted to live so badly. She needed to live for Angel. She needed to live for me." The professor covered his face.

Timothy Lee moved forward to console him.

"Don't you dare," the professor's voice was deep and unsettling. "Don't you dare feign compassion when you have caused this."

"Professor, please hear me. Ask the parent who has lost a child what they would be most thankful for, besides, of course, having that child back. Ask the sibling who has lost a brother or sister what would make them most grateful. Ask anyone who has lost a significant love in their life what they would most cherish. At the end of time, they would all say the same thing: peace, simply peace." The words had no chance of penetrating the professor's mind. "If every prayer was answered and nothing bad ever happened, what kind of love would that breed? Not a strong love. Professor, if I told you that you could have your Sharon back, she would look the same. She would smell the same. She would feel the same. If everything was identical to how you remember her, but - and here's the catch - she was a robot programmed to be just like Sharon. Professor, would that love, if you could call it that, mean as much to you? Would it mean anything to you?"

The professor remained hunched down with his hands on his knees.

"That's the beauty of God's created love. The love He created has a choice. And, if only good things happened to us, that choice would be incredibly easy and therefore not strong at all. You cannot fall in love with a robot, no matter how much it is dressed up and programmed to be like Sharon. It has no choice. Without that choice there is no meaningful love. It is up to us, it is our *freewill* to choose to love God or not. And, because there is freewill, because we decide our choices and actions, there is bad along with good. There has to be good and bad because there has to be a choice." Timothy Lee stopped and studied the professor's face. "Do you understand, professor?"

139

The professor stood from his flexed position. "If I was God and I had the power to do anything, anything at all, I would create love without the tragedy and suffering this ugly life brings. If I could do anything, I would do that."

"I can't argue that with you. All I can say is God really is good. And, rest assure, will answer all of your questions one day. God's mind is so infinitely beyond ours that we could never understand His ways. But, please know they are just and one day you will see how."

The professor backed away from Timothy Lee and kicked dirt on the remaining pieces of chair. "I won't see what isn't there. And there is nothing waiting for any of us but dirt."

Timothy Lee, for the first time, looked exhausted and foiled. "Very well, professor. I guess you have chosen where to put your faith. I can do no more without your help. And I have done all I can to prepare you for the return of your past."

Even as the professor faced away at Taylor's Creek, he could feel Timothy Lee turn and begin walking away. Then, sounding as if it were an inch away, a bird called out, startling the professor. Sitting on the lone rocking chair was a fish crow, which called out its distinct "uh-uh" before flying just over the professor's head. Then, all around, was the feel and sound of nothingness. No breeze brushed against the trees and no crickets played their nighttime song. And up and down Front Street, there were no people and, most notably, no Timothy Lee.

Chapter 29

Jack sat uncomfortably, yet patiently, on the couch as Angel finished getting ready. He knew the professor would not approve of his presence in the house. That, in itself, was enough to make Jack nervous. But, it was also his and Angel's first "real date" which was enough to fill his stomach with a copious supply butterflies. Unbeknownst to both of them, it was actually the *first* date either had ever been on - period.

"Help yourself to anything in the kitchen," Angel yelled out from her bedroom.

"I'm fine, thank you," Jack replied as he stood and walked around the small living room. On a shelf was a cluster of picture frames, some old and some new. The newer pictures showed Angel giving her senior speech in high school and graduating with honors from college. There were pictures of her in rehab holding onto parallel bars as she conditioned her legs. Jack smiled as he examined a family portrait of Angel with her grandmother and the professor. They all had cheerful smiles on their faces, even the professor.

"Sorry it's taking me so long. You okay out there?" Angel's voice made Jack place the picture down quickly.

"Doing just fine. Just looking at some pictures of you and your family. Your grandfather actually looks friendly and approachable in these. I guess those were better times for him."

"They were. He's having a hard time without Grandma around. I don't know. I just worry about him here. This place, this cottage, it's not home to him." Angel ran a brush through her long hair and adjusted her dress so it covered just over her knees.

"I'm not sure anywhere would be home to him now," Jack said before picking up an old photograph. He recognized the young man as the professor. In his lap was a guitar and across from him was a beautiful young lady, whom Jack assumed to be Sharon. "You're grandfather plays the guitar?"

"He used to. My grandma said that's how he won her over. He sang her songs when they were in England together."

"England?"

"Grandpa won a scholarship, the Morehead Scholarship, which covers a semester at Oxford University in England. Grandma also won the award. When they met at Oxford they had no clue they both attended colleges in North Carolina, just a couple of hours from each other. Grandpa attended Wake Forest and Grandma went to Davidson. Anyhow, he played and sang songs and she fell in love. You know those stories: they dated for a month, got engaged and then married in three months time. Then they lived happily ever after until one died. Then the law of love takes over."

"The law of love?" Jack asked, still looking intently at the black and white photo.

"The amount you love somebody, or something, is directly proportional to how much pain they can cause you. I don't like the law, but it's true. The more you love something, the more it's going to hurt at some point. In Grandpa's case, Grandma died."

Jack continued studying the photo. He could not seem to stop staring into the young woman's eyes. He had seen the look before. Not at him, but had seen it in other people's eyes: people walking along the waterfront, sipping coffee together in front of fireplaces, or just sitting in the park together. He knew what the look of love was. Sadly, he could not say he ever saw it in someone he knew. Never did he see it in his parents, what little he could remember seeing of them. He thought that maybe he had seen it in his grandmother's eyes when she looked at a picture or when she was lost in a daydream, but those times were fleeting, if any at all. Without question, Jack could say that he had seen it before. He wondered now if Angel could see it in his eyes.

"Almost ready," Angel's voice stirred Jack back to the present.

"Could he sing?"

"Could who sing?"

"Your granddad."

"Oh yes. Well, he use to. My grandmother said that she fell in love with him the first time he sang to her and kept falling everyday since."

Jack placed the picture back on the shelf. "What song did he sing to her?"

Angel appeared into the room as she answered, "Blue Velvet by…" She looked up at the ceiling trying to remember the name of the singer. "What was his name…?"

Jack could hardly breathe when he turned around. Angel looked like what he could only assume an angel might really look like. She wore a red summer dress that seemed to nestle itself perfectly around her. It drifted just below her knees, tastefully displaying her lower legs that were finished off perfectly with a pair of sandals.

143

"Bobby Vinton," Jack finished.

"That's it!" Angel said, half relieved, but mostly surprised. "You know that song?"

"All too well," Jack managed to say before losing any semblance of a vocabulary. He then lifted his hands as if trying to pull the words from his heart. "You look beautiful."

University of Oxford, England
Forty-four years earlier...

Michael Valentine held his wool jacket over Sharon's head as they ran out of the frigid rain and into the welcomed warmth of the dormitory lobby. For the previous four hours they sat and laughed with their new friends in a dimly lit tavern, called The Eagle and Child, at the same booth C.S. Lewis and J.R.R. Tolkein famously used when they were both at Oxford. Sharon's passion for following the history and stomping grounds of Oxford's most famous residents was contagious to Michael.

"You're soaked," Sharon said as she brushed away a few drops of water from Michael's face.

"There's something about this place that brings out the gallantry in me."

"Does that mean you won't show me gallantry when we get back home?" Sharon asked after nudging Michael with her elbow. She then cut her eyes and smiled.

Back home. Those words struck so deeply. What would he do when he arrived back in North Carolina? Although he tried his best to deny it, he was falling for Sharon in way he had never felt before. And it was not that he did not love Beverly. Certainly he did. But the way he cherished his moments with Sharon were so much more than what he felt with Beverly. It was trite to say, but he felt so much more alive during his weeks at Oxford. He thought it insane, his feelings -- maybe just a temporary infatuation. But, as the days went by, and as his time with her grew, he knew that Sharon was not the woman of his dreams, but instead the woman of his life.

"Checker's in front of the fireplace in ten minutes?" Sharon asked.

"You bring the board and I'll have hot tea ready."

Chapter 30

"Why didn't you pick me up in your truck?" Angel asked as Jack began pushing her down Ann Street.

"And miss this beautiful evening? No way."

Angel looked up at the evening sky and agreed. "I missed it here when I was gone." She reached over her back and placed her hand on Jack's. "Really, I mean it. I missed being here. I missed being here with you. I never imagined that my grandmother wouldn't be around to see me this happy and this content. This summer with you has been almost…," Angel hesitated before using the word. In the back of her mind, she could not stop the thought, the law she knew too well. *The amount you love somebody is directly proportional to the pain they can, and may, cause you.* Everything in her life that she loved ended up causing her great pain: the death of her parents, her ability to walk, her grandmother's death and even part of her grandfather. Everything thing she loved, everything caused pain. So, as her mind said one thing, her heart won out and said another: "magical."

Jack grinned from ear to ear. *Wait until Doug hears this,* he thought to himself.

"So, where are you taking me for dinner?" Angel asked.

"A special place. I think you'll like it."

Jack surprised Angel when he veered her chair toward the ramp at the church. "Why are we stopping here? Did you forget something?"

"Nope." Jack crossed his fingers in hopes that Doug had finished what they had planned. When he opened the front door of the church and pushed Angel through, she saw hundreds of candles illuminating the sanctuary. Shadows waved back and forth upon the walls as the candles flickered almost harmoniously.

"Jack," Angel said before placing her hand over her mouth. "It's beautiful. You did this?"

"It's my way of saying I missed you." Jack stood quiet for a moment, allowing Angel to take in the surroundings.

"It's just so…beautiful."

A blanket lay neatly in front of the Alter, while a covered serving plate sat upon the offering table. Jack lifted the lid. "I hope you like lasagna."

"Oh, Jack. It's my favorite."

After dinner, Jack and Angel laid on the blanket and watched as the candles began burning out, one by one.

"That's kinda how I feel," Jack said as he watched the candle closest to him begin to fade.

Angel lifted her head off Jack's shoulder. "What do you mean?"

"I can't help it. I feel like my day's with you are candles and they're burning away faster and faster."

Angel wrapped her arms around Jack and kissed him. "You know, some candles burn forever."

"Do you think ours will?"

"If it's meant to be, it will."

The church grew dark as the last candle flickered and died. With Jack holding Angel, they both fell into a sleep that was as natural and pure as dew on a blade of morning grass. It was just after midnight that Angel awoke feeling the chill of the cold church. She felt around for the blanket and covered herself and Jack. She then laid her head on Jack's chest and told herself that she would lay there for just a few more minutes. She sighed deeply and listened to his heartbeat as it lulled her back to a peaceful slumber.

Chapter 31

When the professor made it back to the cottage, he noticed a note tied with a string and hanging from his mailbox.

Dear professor,

Farewell my friend…a little verse for you. Sharon knew it well. Philippians 4:6-7. I think you will understand what God gave her and what He has promised those who pray earnestly to him. As for your house, be careful. It appears you might have had some company.

Timothy Lee

The professor shoved the note in his pocket and then walked cautiously to the cottage. He instantly noticed the front door was open and the glass window was broken.

"Who's in here?" he yelled out. "I have a gun and I'll use it."

Buddy and Clover quickly made their way outside to see what the commotion was about. Both were holding baseball bats over their shoulders, ready to strike at a moments notice.

"What happened professor," Clover asked.

"Somebody broke into the house." It was then that the professor thought about Angel being inside. He rushed through the front door and ran back to Angel's room. He turned the light on and saw nothing but an empty bed.

Outside, Clover looked over at Buddy with a confused look on his face. "I'll stay out here in case the robber runs."

"You're just going hide under the porch you big chicken."

"I'm no chicken you little girl."

Buddy placed the bat higher on his shoulder and cocked it in place. "I'll show you a little girl."

Clover took on the same offensive and made his move toward Buddy. "I'm gonna knock your head off you…"

"She's gone," the professor screamed out. "Angel's gone."

Chapter 32

The loud slam of a door awakened Jack and Angel. The church was completely dark, as all of the candles had long burned out.

"What was that?" Angel lifted her head suddenly and surveyed the back of the church.

Jack also jumped to attention and motioned to Angel to duck behind the pew. In the back of the church, no more than 25 yards away, he saw the silhouette of a person moving slowly from the back entrance of the graveyard. "Keep your head down," Jack tried to whisper to Angel, but the acoustic vacancy of the room allowed his voice to carry farther than expected. Jack watched in horror as the figure stood tall and looked in his direction. "I've got to get you out of here," he said before helping Angel into her chair.

"Jack, I'm scared."

"We'll be fine," Jack tried to assure her. "Stay with me and head to the front door."

Angel rolled her chair up the slight incline of the main isle while Jack walked beside her, doing his best to keep sight of the now motionless visitor. Just before Angel reached the knob of the front door, the figure jumped over a pew, into the aisle, and walked hurriedly toward the two. Jack quickly unlocked the door and shoved Angel's wheelchair into the warm night air, made a sharp right turn and held onto the chair as it flew down the ramp. When he had reached a safe distance from the church, Jack slowed the wheelchair to a stop and leaned forward to catch his breath.

"Are you okay?" Angel turned her chair toward Jack and placed her hand on his back.

"I'm okay," Jack managed to say between breaths. "Just a little rattled."

"Who could that have been?"

"I have no idea and I'm not sure I want to find out."

"How did they get in?"

"I must have left the back entrance unlocked."

Angel looked at her watch and showed an obvious increase in concern. "It's 2:30 in the morning. I can't believe we fell asleep like that. My grandpa is probably worried sick."

Jack placed his hands on his hips and looked up at the night sky. "He's gonna kill me. I know he thinks I'm a dirt bag. Now he'll be even more confident of that. I think I'm more scared of him than I am of whoever was in the church."

Angel grabbed his hand. "It'll be fine, but maybe you shouldn't come all the way home with me."

"I'm not going to let you go at this alone. There's no way."

"Just walk me to the house and then I'll go in alone."

Jack walked around in a circle. "No, I may be a lot of things, but I'm no coward."

"Really, you don't have to. Besides, you need to call the police and make sure the church is safe."

After Jack kissed Angel goodnight, she turned toward the house and briefly rehearsed what she would say. Every flood light was on and through the opened window she could see the professor sitting at the kitchen bar, hovering over the phone with his head buried between his hands.

Chapter 33

"I'm sorry," Angel said as soon as her chair made it through the front door. But, what happened next was not at all what she expected. The professor walked straight to her with his hands covering his quivering lips and hugged her tightly.

"I've been worried sick. Where have you been?"

"I'm so sorry, Grandpa," Angel replied. "I've been at the church with Jack. We just lost track of time and fell asleep."

The professor removed his arms from around Angels head and leaned back. The disappointment in his eyes was almost palpable.

"You fell asleep?" The professor glared at Angel and shook his head in a way that only magnified his look of displeasure. "You fell asleep *with* Jack?"

"Grandpa, it's not how it sounds," Angel began. "We were just talking and…"

"You fell asleep," the professor said sharply. "I'm in agony here, worrying myself to the point of insanity, and you are 'falling asleep' with a known convict."

Angel could not help but begin crying. She had never seen this part of her grandfather. He was always in control and a rock for others to stand by. But now, he was weak and scared. He was fragile. He was human.

"It's my fault. I'm the one who stayed with him. And it's not true what they say about him. He didn't commit that crime. He took the blame, Grandpa. He sacrificed his future so his friends could move on with theirs. He's a good person. I know you can't see it, but I do."

The professor stood and stared blankly at Angel. "Someone broke into the house tonight. I thought it was the man who wrote the letters. However, the only fingerprints that showed up were Jack's. He's not an innocent person, Angel. He's a criminal and everyone recognizes that but you."

Angel rolled her chair towards the professor. "He is not a criminal. I had him in the house. He was waiting for me. He must have touched some things but he wouldn't do anything bad. I know him better than that. I know it hasn't been very long, but I know. He's a good person."

"The only fingerprints that didn't belong here are his. And the only thing missing is my medications."

Angel felt her face become warm as she became more frustrated with the professor's accusations.

"He didn't do it. You're just angry at the world and have nothing but bitterness to show it."

The phone rang as Angel turned away and headed for her room. When she answered it, she heard Jack's voice on the other end.

"You'll never guess who our visitor was in the church," Jack began. "Turns out it was a police officer who informed me that I broke into your house and stole some of your grandfather's meds. They're gonna keep questioning me unless you can convince them I didn't do it."

"I know, Jack. I'll get you out. Give me ten minutes and I'll be there."

"No you won't," the professor said with authority. "I want you to stay here and keep the door locked. I'll take care of it. I'll get him out."

Chapter 34

University of Oxford, England
Forty-four years earlier...

Behind Oxford University's Magdalen College lives a field of bright yellow daffodils freckled throughout a blanket of the greenest grass any soul shall likely ever see. It is the field where C.S. Lewis and J.R.R. Tolkein often took walks and discussed their writings. It is also the field where Michael and Sharon cuddled under a Beech tree with leaves the color of plums, and declared to each other that they were in love. And, once those admissions of love were loosed, there was no power on earth that could keep the two apart.

Ironically, it was only three months prior that Michael Valentine had waved goodbye to the woman he, without any question at that time, was madly in love with and anxious to return to after his time in England. But now, as the time to tell her that there would be no wedding and, in fact, no more relationship at all, drew near, he found himself rehearsing how he would tell Beverly. After telling Sharon he was going home to visit his parents for a week, he decided that he would take a couple of days to break the news. Instead, he would lay subtle hints that he hoped would make the admonition less surprising and hopefully less painful. Of course, he was only kidding himself.

"So I'll see you in a week then?"

"Yes, in a week," Michael assured Sharon.

"Is everything okay?" Sharon sensed that Michael had something on his mind. And most certainly, he did.

"Of course," Michael responded. "I'm just wondering how I will go for a couple of weeks without seeing you."

Sharon stepped forward and wrapped her arms around Michael before kissing him. "You just make sure you don't go and find another girl."

Michael tried to laugh but instead closed his eyes and thought of Beverly.

Chapter 35

The professor was the last person Jack expected to see as he left the jailhouse. Yet, when he walked out the front doors, that's exactly who was waiting to drive him back to the church.

"I can walk." Jack shrugged the professor off as if to say no hard feelings.

"I'd prefer you not. I would like to speak with you briefly. We may as well drive."

Jack paused for a moment and then followed the professor to his car. The Volvo appeared new, yet once inside it smelled musty and old. Jack noticed the alterations to aid Angel with getting in and out, in addition to storing her wheelchair in a very accessible back seat. For the first few minutes, nothing was said. But, as the professor made the left down Craven Street, he broke the silence.

"It's nothing personal, Jack. I just don't want you in my house. And here's why: the facts are that I don't know you and your record suggests there are some things a grandfather would be obliged to be concerned about."

Jack looked out the window and exhaled loudly. It was the same broken record he had been hearing since he took the fall for the vandals he once considered his family and friends. "I know it won't change anything, but for the record I'm not a bad kid. I'm not even a criminal. Naïve I am, but a criminal I am not."

The professor stopped the car in front of the church and pulled a checkbook out of his pocket. "Here's a thousand. Once Angel leaves town you'll get another. All you need to do is stay away. Angel has gone through enough hurt and loss in her life. The last thing she needs is to have another." The professor tore the check out and handed it over to Jack. "I hope you can understand."

Jack glared down at the check and, with a frustrated look, shook his head. He then started to open the door but stopped. "You know," he began, "you might think I'm trash and I might, in fact, be trash, but there is not enough money to make me stop caring for Angel."

"Care?" the professor scoffed. "Care, you say. If you cared about her, you would not let her sleep on the floor of this church like some vagabond. If you cared about her, you would not bring her home all disheveled and not even have the decency to see her to the door. You don't know what caring is about and your not about to practice it on my granddaughter."

Jack took the check out of the professor's hand and ripped it in two before he swung his other leg out of the car and slammed the door. He then opened it again and knelt down beside the seat. In a low voice he said, "I may not be what you think is good enough for Angel and I doubt I ever could be. But, this I can promise you: I would never treat Angel the way you treated my grandmother." Jack paused to allow the words to sink in. "You maimed her and you left her." Jack's voice became lower and more staid. "I could never in a million years do that to Angel…Never."

"What on earth are you implying? I don't know your family, nor do I have any desire to."

"Once upon a time you did. Your Beverly was my grandmother."

Chapter 36

The professor felt a sudden wave of nausea as Jack closed the door for the last time and disappeared into the church. He sat there speechless, even to himself. He then laid his forehead against the steering wheel as a thousand thoughts ran through his head. His mind toggled back and forth between belief and disbelief. How could, after all these years, Beverly's life find him? What were the chances of such a coincidence? What were the chances that Jack Dimmer would be her grandson? How did Timothy Lee know? And why did he try to warn him?

The professor sat frozen in his car, hoping that what he just heard was a mistake – that Jack was not really who he claimed to be. As the car idled next to the church, his mind drifted back to that night forty-four years ago.

Wake Forest University, Winston Salem, NC
Forty-four years earlier

Michael Valentine swallowed the lump in his throat and tried once more to break the news to Beverly. The walk along Country

Club Road was lightly populated with other couples whose fates were more promising.

"Beverly, I need to tell you something."

Beverly grabbed Michael's hand and then placed her other arm around his. She then nestled close to him and laid her head upon his shoulder. "What is it, Honey?"

"When I was in England I..." His voice trailed off as another lump found its way into his throat.

"Yes?"

"I thought about us a lot, about our future."

Beverly pulled Michael even closer. "It's exciting isn't it?"

"Well, yes..." But he didn't mean to say that word. No, it was not exciting. It was sad. It was devastating. It was certainly not exciting.

"I know it is," Beverly continued. "But, let's talk about that when we get in the car. I just want to walk and look at the stars. Let's enjoy this moment."

The last ten minutes of that walk seemed like an eternity to Michael. He just wanted to say what he had to say and then run to Sharon. He just wanted to hold her again and start the rest of his life with her. So, when he pulled the car back onto Country Club Road, he gave himself a deadline. As soon as he got off the ramp to Interstate 40, he would just say it. He would just blurt it out and end it. But, as fate would have it, he never made it on that ramp to the interstate...

"Michael, you're going the wrong way," Beverly screamed out just a second too late. Before he could turn his car around, Michael met a bus as it rounded the exit ramp. When he finally regained consciousness, he heard the awful moan from Beverly. "My leg. Oh my God, Michael...my leg."

Chapter 37

The professor knew what he had to do. It was likely what Timothy Lee tried to prepare him for. He turned the ignition off and walked inside the church. Once inside, he saw Jack laying his blanket on the floor.

"Luckily vagabonds are welcomed in this church," Jack said without turning around.

The professor stood in front of the doorway and felt his heart become heavy as he watched Jack get down on his knees, straighten out his blanket and then lay down as if to sleep. Seeing him on the floor of that church made the professor wonder if maybe he had something to do with Jack's homelessness. He walked to the front pew, just a few feet from where Jack laid, and sat down. "Why do you think it's me?"

Jack did not move. "When I was in your house I saw a picture of you playing a guitar. Angel told me you were at Oxford on a scholarship during the time of that picture. My grandmother often talked about a man named Michael. Said she fell in love and almost married him. She talked about how smart he was and that he won a scholarship to a school in England. I'm pretty sure she said Oxford. Anyhow, he was also from North Carolina and attended Wake Forest with her. He sometimes played a Bobby Vinton song for her – Blue Velvet.

She loved it. She was always walking around humming that song."

"I played that for her," the professor admitted.

"After she lost her leg in a car accident, her prince charming evidently didn't like her maimed up body and broke off the wedding with her." Jack sat up and turned to face the professor. "How could you do that? How could you just walk away from her when she needed you so much? You crushed her and you destroyed her life."

"Jack, what I did had nothing to do with her leg. I promise you that. I loved your grandmother. I loved her very much, in fact. But I loved someone else more. I didn't plan to. I guess love does not always follow our plans. That night I was going to tell her about Sharon. I was just about to tell her when the accident occurred."

"I find that difficult to believe. Couldn't you have at least waited until she got out of the hospital? Why did you have to break it off with her cooped up in that bed struggling to come to terms with the fact that she was missing a limb? Good people don't do that. Good people don't hurt someone that badly for their own selfish desires."

The professor leaned forward and rested his arms atop his legs. His head stayed flexed as he spoke. "If I could go back, I would do things differently. You're right. I was selfish. I was selfish and young and madly in love. And when you combine those things, irrational decisions are made. I hid that secret from Sharon. I was always so afraid she would see me differently, that she would not…"

"See you for who you really are?"

"See me for who I really am," the professor agreed.

Jack leaned back with his arms extended. "I'm sure you're not the monster my family thought you were. However, you did ruin my grandmother's life. Man, did she try to overcome her insecurities. However, at the end of the day, she was bro-ken. And, her kids were broken and now here I am to con-tinue the family tradition."

The professor lifted his head and almost found a way to smile. "You're not going to continue what I've started, Jack. I know my Angel, and she won't allow that."

"But you won't allow that, will you?"

"How could I stop her? I only ask one thing of you. Please promise me that you won't hurt my Angel the way I hurt yours."

"Mr. Valentine, I have never had anything positive in my life *except* my grandmother and Doug…until now. I truly care for Angel. I treasure her. I don't mean that I want to run away to Vegas and get married. I treasure her as a friend. It's been a long time since I've had one of those."

The professor held out his hand. "Jack, I'm truly sorry. I hope that you can forgive me."

Jack shook the professor's hand. "Well, unfortunately it's too late for my family. But, I can certainly understand that we make a lot of poor decisions when we're young." Jack then looked the professor in the eyes and said, "I choose to believe you."

After the professor left the church, he drove to the water-front, hoping he might find Timothy Lee there. But, when he got to the spot where they met, he noticed something differ-ent. He found that the two polished rocking chairs were no longer there. Instead, two old and weather-beaten chairs lay upside down in the marsh, looking as if no one had touched them in a hundred years. They were the same rocking chairs the professor saw the first time he came to this spot. For the next hour, he walked along Front Street and at times called Timothy Lee's name. But, it was as if the still of darkness had engulfed any noises and hid them behind steel doors, locked away and dead bolted. There was no rustling of oak limbs or sounds from crows. Only quiet…nothing else.

Chapter 38

For the next three days, the professor walked back to the meeting spot at the west end of Front Street, but still found no signs of Timothy Lee. All that remained were the two weathered chairs turned upside down in the marsh grass. Nowhere in sight were the two gloss white chairs the professor had been accustomed to seeing. He continued waiting for Timothy Lee, hoping he would appear, but to his chagrin, still nothing.

Meanwhile, Jack and Angel continued spending time together with each day bringing stronger feelings for each other. Angel, who strove to open herself up to Jack, allowed him to join her in her daily exercises. However, after the first few days, Angel began questioning if this was such a good idea. Before Jack was with her, she was uninhibited when she screamed out with each forced step while holding herself on parallel bars. She felt less comfortable doing that now as he walked behind her, catching her as she stumbled with every other step.

"It's easier when I'm alone," Angel blurted out, taking Jack by surprise.

"You're doing fine, Angel. I think I've seen an improvement already."

Angel let go of the bars and collapsed to the floor. She covered her face with her hands. "No, I'm not. I'm no bet-

168

ter now than I was eight years ago. I'm not any better and everyone can see it but me. This is not even healthy. I need to put my energy in things that actually matter, things that are actually possible." Angels mascara ran along the bottom of her eyes. "I'm so embarrassed."

Jack knelt down and placed his hands on Angel's face. "The Law of Belief states that what you believe with conviction will become your reality. You taught me that. And you showed me the Law of Concentration. What we concentrate on will, with time, become our reality. And with the Law of Substitution we can replace a negative thought with a positive one because our brain can only hold one thought at a time. So, as you say, 'it might as well be a good thought'. And, my favorite law of all, the one that makes my ears vibrate, is the Law of Attraction. Our thoughts attract our life and those who enter it. That law brought me to you. It changed my life. You've helped me so much, Angel, and I'm not about to let you give up on this. There's no way."

Angel pulled Jack close for a long hug. "I just need a little time alone. I'll be fine. I just need to meditate and get rid of some demons."

"I'll stop by later then?"

"I'll see you then."

After leaving Angel, Jack walked to Front Street and soon found himself sitting in a pristine white rocker looking out across Taylor's Creek. His mind wandered back to Angel and her dream to walk again. He knew this was unlikely, impossible really, after so many years. He only wished he could help more, but he knew this problem was beyond him.

Just as Jack began to relax in the warmth of the sun, a man abruptly sat in the chair next to him. "You scared the life out of me," Jack said as he placed his hand over his chest.

"Well, I certainly do apologize young man. I noticed you enjoying this beautiful day, so I thought I would join you for just a moment."

Jack studied the man's face. He could not place the man, but he knew he had seen him somewhere before. He was a fairly young man, no older than forty-five. His curly brown hair was well trained without a single strand out of place. His face was smooth with freshly shaved cheeks that showcased eyes of piercing, deep green. His expression was alluring and, yet, tranquil. A persistent smile dominated the right side of the stranger's mouth and a faint sparkle made its home in the right eye, as well. Even his impeccably trimmed eyebrows were cared for with the utmost attention. "It is a nice one," Jack said, referring to the weather.

The stranger held a pile of sticks in his hand. He dropped them and then picked one from the ground and tossed it into the creek. "Hasn't rained in three weeks now. The salt is strong, almost like the Dead Sea."

Jack now placed the man. He and Doug came across him a week earlier while taking a walk. The man had mentioned how salty the water was on that day, also.

"They say it's almost impossible for a person to drown in the Dead Sea because the salt concentration makes them buoyant. Even asphalt floats to the surface. That's a strange thing to see."

"Sounds pretty strange," Jack admitted.

"Ever heard of the Dead Sea scrolls?"

"Seems like I have, but I'm not sure."

"It's the greatest discovery in history, yet most people have never heard of it. May I tell you about it?"

Jack had nothing but time to waste until he would see Angel in the afternoon. "Sure."

"Wonderful," Timothy Lee said with enthusiasm. "It all started back in 1947 when a young shepherd boy, an Arab, was exploring the caves around the Dead Sea. In one of those caves, he found an entire library of manuscripts. In fact, there were thousands of them. What made this discovery the greatest in history is the *age* of those manuscripts. Some of these dated back even *before* the time of Jesus! Can't forget that - Jesus wasn't even born. Now," Timothy Lee leaned forward in his chair, "this is important for two reasons. First, the cave contained every book of the Old Testament, except for the book of Esther. This caused, understandably, jubilation among the Christian community. Here's why: people have always doubted the accuracy of the Bible since it was translated in 1611, which is certainly a lot of years since the stories of the Bible took place. In fact, considering that these Old Testament books were written 2000 years after the fact, it makes sense to question their accuracy. People asked the fair question: How can you put any trust in a Book written about things that happened so long ago? Here's what many found unbelievable. The manuscripts were essentially identical to the King James Bible. After nearly 2000 years, the Bible was not mistranslated, not even a little. This simply gave the doubters of the Bible, those who said it couldn't be accurate or trusted because it was written so long after the stories and events happened, a softer foundation on which to stand.

Jack was not nearly as enthusiastic as the stranger telling the story, but he still found the facts somewhat interesting. "That is amazing," he agreed.

The stranger stood from his rocker and peered out into the creek. "There it is," he pointed. "That stick's still floating.

171

Salty, salty, salty, I tell you. You couldn't sink asphalt in it."
He then sat down and rotated his body towards Jack. "Now,
here's what I found so earth shattering about these Dead Sea
Scrolls. As I have already told you, some of these manuscripts
were written before Jesus was even born. And, keep this in
mind, people can't question that a man once lived whose name
was Jesus. Too many different sources written in that time
told about this man called Jesus who called himself the Son
of God. So, you see, it wasn't just the Bible that told of Jesus.
Even those who hated Jesus wrote about Him in their records.
Without question, historically, there lived that Man. What
people do question is if this Person really was whom He said
He was - the Son of God. Was He just a person with great
charisma or was He actually God in human form? Do you
follow me, son?"

Jack nodded his head.

Timothy Lee flashed a broad smile. "You've got it. Now,
listen to this. In these texts that validate the Old Testament, it
tells about the coming of a great Man. It said that He would
be born in Bethlehem and would ride into Jerusalem on a
donkey." The stranger leaned forward and pulled an old tat-
tered Bible from beneath his chair. He then thumped it with
his hand, like an old school preacher. "Guess who was born in
Bethlehem and who rode into Jerusalem on a donkey?"

"Jesus," Jack answered, even though the question was rhetorical. The stranger's enthusiasm seemed almost manic.

"That's correct. It also said that a friend would betray
Him. Remember Jesus was betrayed by His friend, Judas?
The Old Testament said His enemies would wound him and
they would pierce His hands and feet. They did that to Jesus.
It said 30 pieces of silver would be exchanged for His delivery
to the enemy and that the price for His life would be used to
buy a potters field. It's right here." (He thumped the Bible
again) "It comes true in the New Testament. That's what they

did to Jesus! They sold him for thirty pieces of silver and then used the money to buy a potters field. Isn't that fascinating?"

Jack nodded his head. The stranger's seemingly overreaction was making things grow uncomfortable.

It says that He would be crucified among thieves, His clothing would be gambled upon, He would be pierced in the side and through all His beatings, not a single bone would be broken. Sound familiar? All this before the Man we call Jesus was even born. It said He would be buried in a rich man's tomb but that His flesh would not rot and that after He was crucified, the earth would become dark, even though it is day." Timothy Lee took a moment to let his rants be absorbed. "My new friend, what are the chances of all these prophecies coming true?"

"Mister, I live in a church."

"I know where you live. And I know that heavy stick is still floating in that creek behind you."

"Why do you keep telling me that?"

"I think you should know."

Jack was perplexed. "Thank you, I know quite well now. Another question…"

"You want to know why I keep dropping this pile of sticks, don't you?"

"Actually, yes."

"Someone once told me that this world -- this world that is unimaginably fine tuned for our survival -- is simply an accident. They told me that given enough time, billions of years, everything could fall in place to allow life to form with an environment to support it."

"What does that have to do with dropping sticks?"

"Everything and nothing. You see, when I was a child my adoring grandfather sat down with me, and together we made a house out of sticks. It was such a lovely house. It had two windows in the front, two in the back, a functioning door and a chimney. I loved it. It even had a little kitchen table inside. Well, I lost that house when my real house caught fire. And, how I wish I could build a little house like that again. I miss it terribly." Timothy Lee moved his hand out and made a panoramic arc, as if to reveal everything around him. "So, here is my experiment, I figure that if all of this could happen by chance, by accident, then surely there is a chance that if I keep dropping these sticks, eventually they will fall in place, just the right way, and a house will be made – all by accident."

Jack nodded his head out of respect for his life.

"Whathcha think? Do you think there's a chance that these sticks will eventually fall together and, by accident, form a house like my grandfather made for me? I know you're thinking no. But, what if I had chance to drop them for a million years? How about a billion years? A trillion? Do you think there would be any chance this could happen?"

Jack said nothing.

"Me neither," Timothy Lee answered, "but I'm gonna keep trying out of respect for my friend, because he tells me the earth and universe were made by accident. And, by golly, there's a far better chance that these sticks will accidentally fall in place and form a house, than the universe being created by accident. Nobody would refute that. And, you know, you have to wonder. Where did the stuff come from that supposedly made...," Timothy Lee again pointed to his surroundings, "this stuff?"

Jack shrugged his shoulders.

"It comes down to one question: where's your faith? Because, no matter which one you choose to believe, either science or the word of the Bible, it takes faith."

Jack's discomfort around the stranger grew intolerable. Something felt wrong, maybe just creepy, but also inhuman. "Well, sir, I appreciate the conversation but it's getting late and I have plans to meet someone."

Timothy Lee rocked back and smiled. "She doesn't expect you until later, Jack."

Jack's skin crawled. His muscles became taut, his mouth dry, and he knew for certain something about this person was dreadfully wrong. It was altogether possible that this man could have guessed it was a girl and that the date would not take place until dinnertime – like most dates young people have. But, what shook Jack was the stranger knew his name. So, when he finally found his voice, he asked, "Do you know me?"

"Of course, you're Jack Dimmer. You were once accused of vandalizing the Ann Street Church." Timothy Lee then leaned close to Jack and studied his eyes. They blinked wildly. "But, I don't buy it. I don't believe you were raised that way."

Jack said nothing.

"Let's take a walk, what do you say? Then you can hurry off to meet the young lady."

Jack, still stunned, sensed it would not be wise to decline the offer.

Chapter 39

The professor opened the last note from Timothy Lee and again read the scripture. He could not seem to remember exactly which one it was.

"Philippians 4:6-7," he whispered to himself before folding the note and calling out for Angel. "Angel, sweetie, could you tell me again what your grandmother said before she…" He did not need to finish the sentence.

Angel removed the deep muscle stimulators from her thighs and then rolled into the living room. "Grandpa, why do you keep asking me that question?" Her voice was not agitated, only concerned.

"I can't seem to remember the details of it. I just can't seem to pay attention."

Angel felt confident the professor's forgetfulness was only a defensive mechanism. These changes in people are quite common when they go through a particularly painful loss. "She said to tell you she felt at peace. She called it an 'incredible peace.'"

The professor said nothing, but instead read the verse to himself once more.

Don't worry about anything; instead, pray about everything.

Tell God what you need and thank him for all he has done.

If you do this you will experience God's peace, which is far more wonderful than the human mind can understand.

His peace will guard your hearts and mind as you as you live in Christ Jesus. (Philippians 4:6-7)

The professor sat back and read Timothy Lee's note again:

Dear professor,

Farewell my friend - just a little verse for you. Sharon knew it well. Philippians 4:6-7. I think you will understand what God gave her and what He has promised those who pray earnestly to him. As for your house, I assure you that I had nothing to do with this.

Timothy Lee

The news hit Buddy hard. Where did he do wrong? He was at the senior center playing pool when he first heard – Louise was newly in love, engaged and soon to be married. How did he let her slip through his hands? He should have known his meal ticket was out of date. Louise had not cooked for him in two weeks. But, how did she decide so suddenly? What did Clover do to persuade her? "That pencil-head," he thought. However, the hardest truth to accept was that he would miss his charades with Clover. They had been going at it for so many years. Now Clover would lounge all day in Louise's recliner, rubbing his tummy and picking out pieces of food from his teeth just so he wouldn't miss one tiny piece of that home-cooked heaven. "Pencil-head," he sputtered again before falling face-first on the couch and covering his head with a pillow.

Just after Buddy walked through the front door of his house and mourned the news of Louise's future without him, Clover trampled through his back door, grabbed a bad of Fritos and a Pepsi, and then cried and sulked his way to the bathroom. He sat, fully clothed, on the toilet and began stomping the floor like a sprayed roach. He was barely able to catch a breath of air between sobs. He had heard the news in the courthouse yards, where he was doing community service for stealing Maggie-the-dog from the nice young couple down the street. He should have known something was wrong when Louise didn't cook for him for two weeks. How could Buddy have stolen her in such a sprinkle of time? Where did he go wrong? And, as if things couldn't be worse, he found himself missing the future skirmishes with his lifelong nemesis. Sure, Buddy nearly killed him with that hole-in-the-porch move earlier in the summer, but, well, he didn't. "Dirt mouth," Clover whimpered. He then shoved a handful of chips down his throat and chugged the Pepsi. "Dirt mouth."

Chapter 40

"Certainly is a beautiful afternoon. If only we could know how much of a gift these times are." Timothy Lee locked his fingers behind his head and bathed in the sun's warmth. "Ever hear of a Rhesus monkey, Jack?"

"I can't say I have."

"Smart little monkeys. If I didn't know better, I'd almost believe that we really are evolutionary siblings. Do you know why?"

Jack found himself watching every word, being careful not to anger the man. "Because they're intelligent like we're suppose to be?"

"No, because they act unenlightened like we do. These little monkeys were so smart that they were nearly impossible to trap. So, what scientists did was anchor down some bottle-neck soda-pop containers and placed a nut in the bottom of them. Now, when those Rhesus monkeys saw these nuts they put their arms and hands through the opening and grabbed a hold of them. Unfortunately, for them, when they tried to pull their hands out, they wouldn't fit because the nut was too big. Here's where we are alike: instead of just letting go of that nut and pulling their hand out, thus becoming free, they refused to let go. When they didn't let go, the scientists simply captured them."

Jack nodded his head inferring that he understood.

"Many times we act the same as those monkeys. We refuse to let go of a part of our past that is holding us back. You understand what I'm saying, Jack?"

Jack suddenly felt more comfortable. Maybe the stranger was not as shady as he seemed. Maybe he really was trying to help. Besides, he was walking Jack back to the populated business row of Front Street, not out to some secluded area where he could harm or rob him. "I understand, thank you."

"So, I assume that you will learn from these monkeys and get on with your life?"

Jack smiled at Timothy Lee. "I already am."

"Good, because somebody special is out there waiting for you and I'd hate to hear that you let her go."

Jack again fought off the unsettling feelings and told himself that, even though the stranger knew too much about him, he seemed to be genuinely interested in his well-being. Even so, Jack walked quietly with Timothy Lee, not knowing the true identity of his newfound friend.

"You believe in evolution?"

Jack felt a little more comfortable and decided to make light. "Not after hearing how dumb those monkeys are."

Timothy Lee did not seem to catch the joke. "Darwin, assuming you know who he is, wasn't an evil man. When he became a young man, he studied many subjects, nature being just one of those. What bothered him greatly was the cruelty he saw. He questioned how a benevolent God could allow wild animals to mangle another, torturing them inhumanly before feeding on them. In particular, he studied a wasp that would drive its dagger into a caterpillar or grasshopper, over, and over, with no intent to even eat it. Instead, it placed larvae inside the insect that then matured and ate its way out of the slowly dying creature. He wondered why a cheetah had to drive its claws and fangs into a helpless antelope and then hold its throat in its jaws until the poor animal quit jerking."

"How would Christians respond to that?" Jack asked.

"They would respond truthfully. They would answer that they do not know. I didn't know. When I saw everything that I loved fall apart and die without mercy and in complete innocence, those questions and doubts tried to get to me. And, I had no answers, at least no enlightening ones. All I had was faith. I had to fight for belief in God. I had to fight for belief that He was something altogether good. Faith isn't an easy thing, Jack. As Darwin found, it's nearly impossible at times. But, in my position, I can tell you this about the cruel world of nature and animals in particular. Many Christians write animals off as not being as important as we are. Mainly because we think we are made in God's image. But, let me tell you something about animals. God doesn't create stuff just for the sake of creating it. And he certainly doesn't create something as loyal and loving as a dog, or other pet, only to have it banished away."

"So why are some animals so dangerous and vicious?" Jack asked.

Timothy Lee scratched his forehead. "Why are some people so dangerous and vicious? Jack, when sin entered this world it became like a virus; like a cancer. Sin is the worst virus to ever enter this world. It's much worse than even the Ebola virus. When Ebola enters our body, it causes cells to burst and bleed. Blood runs from our mouth, our ears; it even causes us to cry tears of blood. Then it spreads, seemingly uncontrollable, from one victim to the next, until untold thousands die. But then, without reason, it burns itself out and stops. Sin is not like that. Sin continues to spread and becomes more and more destructive. Everything is affected -- us, our crops and food sources, our greed, and, to answer your question, the animals. As sin permeated every corner of our life and surroundings, it caused diseases to increase, such as cancer, and it caused the world – the animals – to become more cruel and merciless. But that will all change when the Lord returns. One of my favorite verses is Isaiah 65:25." Timothy Lee again fanned through the aged Bible in his hand until he found the verse. He then cleared his voice and read, "The wolf and the lamb shall feed together, and the lion shall eat straw like the bullock: and dust shall be the serpent's meat. They shall not hurt nor destroy in all my holy mountain, saith the Lord." Timothy Lee closed the Bible and placed it firmly under his arm. "Can you imagine when a lion will eat straw instead of other animals? Darwin couldn't see this. He couldn't see, at least from what we know, that sin was the cause of wasps torturing caterpillars and cheetah's tearing into antelope. Maybe no one bothered to mention the possibility of such truths."

Jack watched as his feet stepped over each line in the concrete sidewalk. He listened intently to the stranger's rants.

"Darwin believed this was all an accident. He believed that one day science would show that life as we now see it, evolved slowly, piece by piece, and small changes at a time. He believed that we would one day see the evidence that transitions have happened slowly, until maybe even the primates, such as the Rhesus monkey, evolved into you and me. But, here's what your world now knows…"

My world? Jack thought. *Isn't it his world, too?*

"Look down at your feet, Jack. This is what today's archaeology has found. With every line that you step across, imagine that the space until the next line represents around twenty million years. Now, let's walk." With each line that was crossed, Timothy Lee would say, "Nothing yet. No advanced life." After passing over a hundred yards of lines, Timothy

Lee puts his arm out and stops Jack dead in his tracks. "After all the digging, after all the hundreds of millions of years of history, suddenly in a span of one of these spaces, between two lines, around forty new body types are found. It's called the Cambrian explosion because, well, there's an explosion of life. Keep in mind, there is no transition period leading to this. Darwin's evolution says that there are *no* sudden leaps in nature. It says there are transitions that slowly lead to mankind. Yet, in the Cambrian explosion, everything shows up suddenly – at once."

"That's very convincing," Jack remarked.

"No it's not," Timothy Lee replied. "Not to everyone. People will continue to find ways to prolong this debate."

"Well, what do you believe?" Jack asked, confused by the stranger's parables.

"I have an advantage, I know the truth. But, you do not."

Jack figured the jury was in. This was a nice guy, seemed to really care, but, in the end, a definite head case. "So, what do I take from this?"

"Faith has to do with things you cannot see and belief in things you cannot hold in your hand."

"I see."

"No you don't," Timothy Lee corrected him. "You can't see; you can only have faith." He then handed Jack the worn Bible he had been using.

"What's this for?"

"Return it to its owner. You know him well."

Jack opened the cover and saw the name Sharon inscribed in it. "This is Mr. Valentine's…"

"Yes it is," Timothy Lee confirmed. "And, Jack, that stick is still floating."

Before Jack could say another word, the stranger sprinted away, skipping and tapping his heels as he went. A couple then walked by talking about the forecast for rain in the evening. It was at that moment that the stick made sense to Jack. He clutched the Bible and ran off in the opposite direction.

Chapter 41

Jack's heart was racing when he finally arrived to the front door of the cottage. For him, it was the first real chance to help change someone's life for the better.

"Jack, is everything okay?" The professor noticed that Jack looked frazzled and nervous as he stood at the front door.

"Mr. Valentine, everything is great. I just need to see Angel a little earlier than planned."

"She's in the shower right now, but she should be out directly. Why don't you come in and have a seat."

"Thank you." Jack held the Bible in front of him. "It was a strange encounter, but a man gave me this to give back to you."

The professor noticed the Bible immediately. He opened the front cover and ran his finger across Sharon's name. "Jack, I need to ask you something and I don't mean to anger you. This man who gave you the Bible, do you two know each other?"

The question confused Jack. "No, never, I was just sitting in a chair near Taylor's Creek when he came up to me. He preached to me and took me on a walk. Before he left, he handed me this Bible."

"The chair, was it an old rocking chair or a new one?"

Jack had not paid particular attention to the chair, but when he thought back, he did recall it being quite shiny. "It was pretty new. What does that have to do with anything?"

"It's complicated. Jack, the man who gave this to you is named Timothy Lee. Before I knew that Beverly was your grandmother, he warned me that my past with her was coming back. He knew about you. So, I need to know. How would he know that? How would he know that you were Beverly's grandson, that I was engaged to her and, finally, that I would meet you?"

The subtle accusation bewildered Jack. "I don't know how he would know all that about me or you. This is just plain weird. I had no idea who Timothy Lee was until now."

"What are you two talking about?" Angel sat in the hallway, her hair dripping wet. Her eyes were inquisitive and confused as she looked at the professor. "What about you and Jack's grandmother? Engaged?"

The professor creased his lips and looked down at the floor.

"Nothing, really," Jack said in an attempt to brush the conversation aside. "I was just talking about her. I was just saying how I wished Mr. Valentine could have known her."

Angel remained suspicious of the momentary discomfort in the room, but allowed Jack's answer to suffice. "Why are you early, Jack?"

"There's something I need to show you and it just can't wait."

Angel looked back and forth at the professor and Jack. She knew something was amiss. It was palpable in the air. "What's going on here?" The professor remained speechless. "Are you guys not telling me something?"

Jack glanced over at the professor before answering, "We're telling you that you need to come with me. Really, I need you to come."

"I need to dry my hair first. It'll only take a few minutes."

"That won't be necessary."

Jack and Angel's walk to Front Street was uncharacteristically quiet. Jack's thoughts were preoccupied with the event that was about to take place. Angel was trying to make sense of the conversation she walked into. Nonetheless, when they arrived at Taylor's Creek, Jack noticed two distinctive things. One, the rocking chairs were now faded and turned upside down, just beyond the marsh grass. And, second, the creek was perfectly flat, without a wave. The surface looked almost like glass, sending any ray of light skipping across the salty water. Above the horizon of trees, the sun began settling in, melting away into pink and purple striations against a still Carolina blue sky. Jack felt a peace about the moment. He also felt the unfamiliar chance to make someone else's life better.

"Jack, why are we here? This is exactly where my grandfather asked me not to go."

Jack was undeterred. He stepped behind the wheelchair and pushed Angel through the centipede grass until they reached the marshy banks of the creek. "You have to trust me." Jack walked around the chair and knelt in front of Angel. He stared her in the eyes with a passion she had never seen or felt before. "I need to do this, Angel. You and I being here was not my idea. It came from somebody else, somebody I don't know, but who I feel has led me to this spot with you.

I listened. I listened for the good in what I thought was a bad situation. Do you understand me?" Jack held Angels hands against his chest. "I made myself expect something good. Before you came into my life, I would have never done that." Jack stood and held Angels hands firmly. He then pulled her toward him and lifted her from the chair.

"Jack, are you sure you haven't lost your mind? Tell me you're not taking me into that creek."

Jack walked briskly to the water's edge and stopped to say a brief prayer. "If that's what you want to hear but…" Jack sloshed through the marshy shore and then quickly found the water up to his waste.

"Jack, please, I've been in pools hundreds of times." Angel slapped Jack's back to make him stop wading any farther out. "I still can't walk, Jack. Don't do this to me. I'm tired of failing. So, please…" Tears of frustration ran down her cheeks and she buried her head in Jack's shoulder. "Please take me back." Angel was as disheartened as she had ever been. She was tired of trying; tired of the letdowns. She just wanted to lie down and cry.

Jack's heart ached as he heard Angel's words, but he knew he had to do this. He would regret it if he never tried. "Hold onto my shoulders. I'm letting you down."

Angel clutched firmly to Jack, fearful that she would sink if she did not. As soon as her trunk entered the water, she knew something about this felt drastically different. It seemed as if the water pushed against her, like two magnets of the same pole pushing away from each other. Her feet hit the bottom and she felt the pressure of them against the sand. Jack said nothing, but held onto Angel's elbows in case she collapsed. She lifted her eyes to Jack's and, in complete astonishment, moved her arms away from his.

Jack kept his eyes on Angel's. He wanted to savor every second. He wanted to see that sparkle in her eyes that he had envisioned while he was running to her house. He wanted to see the moment, the happiest moment of her entire life. And, on that night, he would.

"Jack, oh my God," Angel said before her lips began to quiver. "I'm standing. I'm standing, Jack."

Jack's heart burst with emotions. He was doing something good for someone. He was opening a part of her life that no one would have ever done. So, he stepped back a few yards and smiled broadly. "Okay, now take a step."

"Jack, I'm not sure I can."

"You can. I know without a doubt. On this night, a night you will never, ever forget, you will walk; if not for yourself, then for me…"

Before Jack could even finish his sentence, Angel contracted the muscles in her stomach and pushed her right leg forward. She lost her balance momentarily, but the buoyancy of the water held her upright. She then pushed her left leg and followed it again with her right.

"Angel," Jack said softly as she took another step through the creek, "You're walking."

Happy tears continued running down Angel's cheeks. She sniffled, then laughed, then cried, and then sniffled again. She looked up at Jack. "I'm walking."

Jack stopped walking backwards and allowed Angel to reach him. When she did, she placed her hands on both sides of his face and kissed him. And, as the faintest glow of the now slumbering sun gave Jack a final glimpse of Angel's eyes, she pulled him to her and pressed her chest against his. "Jack Dimmer, you've made me the happiest girl in the world." She then pushed him away so she could look directly at him. "I love you, Jack. I just love you so much. I do." She then pulled him close again and held him for what seemed a lifetime. Jack savored the feeling; a feeling he had never felt before and would possibly never feel again. If it all ended at that moment, his life would be complete. But, instead, the feeling would last most of the night, as Angel walked up and down Taylor's Creek, watching the stars as she went. And, she would continue doing so far beyond the midnight hour, as the rest of the world slept.

Later that evening, across town at a sketchy apartment complex, two men exchanged gifts: money for one and drugs for the other. Timothy Lee strongly coveted these two gifts. But, that desire was quickly remedied after he placed a bullet in one of the men's head, and then another bullet in the other man's chest. He then scoured the corpses like a hungry animal. He walked away with a pocket full of cash and a jacket full of crack cocaine. It ended up being a wonderful evening for him, as well.

Chapter 42

When Angel awoke, the professor was just coming in from an early morning walk. He made his way into the kitchen, poured a cup of coffee and then walked back outside without saying a word. She assumed, of course, that he was upset with her for staying out so late. But, that was not the case at all. He was preoccupied with something he never expected to happen; something he never thought he would have to do. Regardless, Angel just knew he would be ecstatic once he learned of the reason for her late return. So, after she topped off her coffee with heavy cream, she pushed her way to the front porch.

"Grandpa, I know you're upset, but you need to know why I was out late."

"I'm not upset with you," the professor said before Angel could tell him the news. "You're an adult and I need to respect that." He then took a sip of his coffee and looked over at her. "Angel, there's something you need to know about Jack and his grandmother and, most importantly, me."

Wake Forest University Baptist Medical Center, Winston Salem, NC
Forty-four years earlier

All Michael Valentine knew was that he was in madly in love and he simply could not imagine a life without Sharon in it. He just could not bare the thought. And, after two nights of sleeplessness and two days of pretending he still loved Beverly the same as before his time at Oxford, he had to rid himself of the torture. He had to tell her. He was not naïve as to how painful this would be for himself and, even more so, Beverly. All he knew was he could not pretend anymore. Sharon was to arrive the next day and he wanted everything to be right. However, his timing would haunt him the rest of his life. And, as for Beverly, it would turn a bright future into mental and physical struggles. It would replace her house in a ca-du-sac with a loving husband and polite children into a broken down trailer, with part-time electricity, sagging floors, two abusive husbands, and a child who overdoses on heroin and leaves behind a son named Jack. If Michael Valentine knew the sequence of events that would lead to Beverly's altered life, even his love for Sharon would have been sacrificed. Unfortunately, life does not give one that chance.

"This is not the time, Michael," Beverly's father argued. "She's lying in that bed with a missing leg and the last thing she needs to hear is that you don't want to be her husband anymore."

"It's not what it seems. I'm in love with someone else. I didn't plan it to be this way. I can't live this lie any longer. It's not even fair to her."

Beverly's father stepped closer to Michael and deepened his voice. "Fair to her? Look you spineless coward. It is bad enough you maimed my daughter's body and that you now want to do the same to her heart. But, to lie on top of it all," *he shook his head in disgust,* "I never thought you were capable."

"I'm not telling you a lie," Michael protested.

"You're not going in that room with the intentions you have right now, young man."

Michael wanted to break down and agree, but he knew he couldn't leave without coming clean. *"I have to tell her."*

"Over my dead body."

"Then you'll have to tell her yourself." *Michael Valentine turned and walked away.* *He planned to never look back.*

Forty-four years later, he would have to...

"If I could only go back, Angel, I would do it so differently. But, I just couldn't bare your grandmother finding out that my fiancé was laying in a bed with an amputated leg and that I wanted to leave her. Sharon would have walked away. She's not like me; she's a better person than that."

Angel dropped her head. Her mind could not help but notice the cracked and broken paint on one piece of the porch and the untarnished board just next to it. The power of the moment overtook all the teachings of a positive mindset. The poisoned thoughts covered her body and she knew the reality that confronted her. Everything in her life that she ever loved left her broken hearted; every chapter that she had ever lived, ended in tragedy. Now, it appeared the same would happen. The curse would live on, unless she could figure out a way to stop it.

"So, Jack knew before we left last night? And, that's the conversation I overheard?"

"Yes. We talked and he just wanted to hear the truth. This won't change your friendship with him at all."

"Grandpa, how could it not? Right now he may be okay with it, but as time goes on and it continues to live inside him, he will change."

"He said he felt selfish for even implying that everything worked out the wrong way, but had it not, he wouldn't be here to meet you. He said that you were the best thing to ever happen to him."

"Grandpa, I believe you when you said you would have done things differently if you could go back, but the truth is things are what they are. So, considering Jack's life, me being the best thing to happen in it, really doesn't say much."

The professor held his head down. He knew there was no way to make his past with Beverly anything close to trivial. Somehow, over the years, he managed to keep his focus on Sharon, instead of his past with Beverly. Now, that would be impossible.

Angel could not bare to see the pain in her grandfather's eyes. She rolled up to him and wrapped her arms around him. "It's okay. What you did was not your fault."

The professor looked up. "How could you say that? Of course, it was my fault."

"First, you were young, which means you were unwise. Second, you were in love. And, love has blinded every person who has ever been in it. No one can ever say they didn't make a poor decision because of that desire for love. Except for Jesus, of course."

The professor managed a smile. "Now you sound like your grandmother."

"I know you don't believe this, but God has never seen a mistake that we can make, that he can't use for some greater good. I'm not paralyzed because of what happened to Jack's grandmother. But, in a way, I have walked again because of what she raised, or maybe I should say 'who she raised'."

"What are you talking about?"

"Well, did you know it is almost impossible for someone to drown in the Dead Sea…"

Chapter 43

The afternoon brought with it a peace in the professor's heart that had been absent since Timothy Lee first reminded him of Beverly. He even felt better that Angel now knew the truth. Whatever future she and Jack had together, it was necessary that she know the identity of his grandmother. Even so, the professor was relieved to learn what Jack did for Angel and the obvious intent he had to bring joy to her life. Even considering the circumstances, Jack's heart was in the right place.

His mind clear, the professor walked along Craven Street, listening to the cadence of the locus, the passing drone of bees and the announcement of dusk by the local chorus of grasshoppers. When he reached Front Street, he noticed something that made his heart stop beating: the rocking chairs were once again gleaming and new. They sat beneath the oak tree, one facing the other as if two people had been sitting knee-to-knee. Nowhere in sight were the dated and chipped chairs. Even so, the professor sat on the nearby bench and simply stared at the pristine rockers.

Before long, a familiar truck arrived. It inclined to one side, causing its shocks to take issue with the weight of the driver. Diesel stepped out and removed his Oakley sunglasses before peering out across the creek. Once the vehicle righted itself, Chance and Dillon exit it. On Dillon's face was a pair of miniature, matching sunglasses that he also removed and copied Diesel's actions. However, once the child noticed the professor, he ran across the grassy shoreline and jumped into the professor's arms. Taken by surprise, the professor was unsure of how to react to such a show of affection. Even so, he managed to give Dillon a soft hug.

"Mr. Michael, look what Mr. Diesel bought me." Beaming, he held his sunglasses up for the professor to see and then placed them on his face. After modeling them for a moment, he asked if he could sing a song. The professor knew the song well now, as Dillon made sure he sang it at least three times during each of their meetings.

"You know what song I'd like to hear, Mr. Dillon?"

Dillon jumped up and down. He could barely contain his excitement that someone would actually make a request. "Tell me, tell me. I'll sing it good."

The professor leaned back and crossed his legs. "I'd love to hear Jesus loves me."

Dillon clapped his hands and began singing. Chance sat beside the professor and patted him on the back. "I should probably teach him another song."

"I like this one just fine."

In the distance, as Dillon sang, Timothy Lee hid behind some landscaped bushes and watched intently. He studied Chance and the professor some, but kept the brunt of his attention on the child with the angelic voice. He smiled and hummed along. He whispered to himself, "What a precious child. What a precious, precious child."

When Dillon left with Diesel and Chance, the professor left his seat on the bench and found his way to the rocking chairs. In his hands, he carried Sharon's Bible. He hoped that if he read a verse aloud, it would summons the wise stranger whom he had not seen in what seemed like months. But, before he could even lift the leather cover of the book, a voice stopped him from behind.

"May I suggest a verse to you?"

"Timothy Lee," he gasped. "I've been looking for you."

"I'm assuming you and Jack have become more acquainted?"

"How did you know?"

"You need to have faith that I knew for the right reasons. Now, I'm glad you invited me back."

"How'd you know I wanted to see you back?"

"Well, you just told me, of course. How else would I know?"

The professor missed the humor in Timothy Lee's response. "It just seems like you know everything."

"I only know what I am told." There was a long silence before Timothy Lee continued. "So then, turn Sharon's Bible to Exodus 14:21."

The professor fumbled through the pages but could not seem to locate the requested chapter.

"May I," Timothy Lee held his hand out. The professor submitted and handed the Bible to him.

Like a professional poker player, Timothy Lee fanned through the pages. "Here we are. *And Moses stretched out his hand over the sea; and the Lord caused the sea to go back by a strong east wind all that night, and made the sea dry land, and the waters were divided.*" He slid his finger a few verses down to the twenty-eighth verse. "*And the waters returned, and covered the chariots, and the horsemen, and all the host of Pharoah that came into the sea after them; there remained not so much as one of them.* Do you recognize these verses, professor?"

"The story of Moses parting the Red Sea, of course."

"Well, actually, God did that part for Moses. But, why did He?"

"He was fleeing from an army."

Timothy Lee appeared pleased with the answer. "Very good. The Israelites were fleeing the mighty Egyptian army. When they came to the Red Sea, God parted it and allowed His people to cross. However, when the Egyptians followed suit, the walls of water crushed back together, thus drowning the army. I want you to remember that the army used horses and chariots."

"I remember," the professor acknowledged. "But why are you telling me this story?"

"I'm telling you this story because I want you to believe in miracles. I want you to have faith that you can have the miracle of seeing your wife again."

The professor shook his head and looked away before saying, "I can't."

Timothy Lee walked forward and placed his hand on the professor's shoulder. "I know you can't. But, although you have not admitted it, I know you're trying to. And that's all God needs. He needs to know you're trying."

"It's just impossible."

"So many things are. The sequence of events that have placed you here are impossible, at least in human terms."

"I'm sorry. But, I can't have faith that I will see her again."

"All things are possible through the Lord, Michael Valentine." Timothy Lee removed his hand from the professor's shoulder and then placed it gently against his cheek. He then looked down at the professor's watch. "It's nine o'clock. I have to go now. There are other things to attend to."

199

"Will I see you again?"

"Not here," Timothy Lee said as he began walking away.

"Please tell me who you are."

Timothy Lee acknowledged the question with a sympathetic nod. "When the time is right, you will know." He then turned and sprinted away.

At approximately quarter past nine, Timothy Lee entered the home of an elderly couple who were just getting ready for bed. He shot them both, took their medications, and left them to die. Within a few minutes, they did just that.

Chapter 44

When the professor arrived home, he placed Sharon's Bible on the coffee table and then sat back in his recliner. He was running the conversation with Timothy Lee through his mind when he noticed some papers stuck inside the Bible. He opened the book and pulled out the sheets. There were some pictures of, what appeared to be, coral-covered spoked wheels and bones, at the bottom of the sea or ocean. Some of the bones were obviously human remains, but others appeared much larger. The professor sat the pictures to the side and then opened a single piece of folded paper. It was a letter from Timothy Lee.

Dear Professor,

I hope you find the photos interesting. What you're looking at are remnants found at the bottom of the Red Sea, a few years back. Many believe the wheels, which obviously have spokes, to be those of the Egyptian army. Some years ago, in the late seventies, a gentleman by the name of Richard Rives brought a chariot wheel (from the bottom of the Red Sea) to the surface. Nassif Mohammed, who was the director of Antquities in Cairo, examined the wheel. Mohammed dated the wheel back to the times of the Egyptian army – the 18th Dynasty of ancient Egypt. The wheel had eight spokes. This is an important observation because only the Egyptian dynasties from around 1400 B.C. used wheel hubs with eight spokes. This matches the period of the parting of the Red Sea. So, the question is, how did these remnants get to the bottom of the Red Sea? Could it be that these are the remains of the Chariots that pursued Moses and the Israelites?

WorldNetDaily interviewed a Swedish scientist by the name of Lennart Moller, from the Karolinska Institute in Stockholm. This respected scientist stated that there is also evidence of the remains of ancient human and animal skeletons. Now, what he says about this is certainly fair from a scientific standpoint. He states that, 'There was a disaster [there] a long time ago. Whatever that is, it's open to interpretation'.

So, professor, considering these evidences and the pictures you have in front of you, one has two choices. One, they may choose to have faith it means nothing. Or, two, they may choose to have faith these discoveries support one the greatest and most popular miracles in the Bible. The question remains, professor – where's your faith?"

I have enjoyed my time with you.

Farewell,

Timothy Lee

Chapter 45

Clover and Buddy sat on their front porches, neither acknowledging the other. Both knew, or at least assumed, that a congratulation was in order for the other. It was over, each thought, no more home cooked meals. No more competition. No more future with Louise. It was only when the sweet aroma of blueberry cobbler drifted across the street, along with the sound of flirtatious laughter, that the two dejected men faced each other.

"Who's your future wife cooking with over there?" Clover asked first.

"My wife?" Buddy shot back. "I heard the news. I know what you've done. You just want rub it in, don't ya?"

Clover's face became distorted. "What are you talking about?"

"What am I talking about? What are you talking about?" Buddy's face always looked a little distorted.

Before the conversation became any more unfruitful, Louise opened her front door, walked out giggling, and disheveled. When she saw her forlorn ex-eaters, she quickly patted down her hair and untwisted her dress. But, as much as she tried, love would not allow her to keep a straight face. She began giggling uncontrollably, like a first crush schoolgirl. Then behind her appeared the great mystery of her giddiness.

"UNCLE FRANK?" Buddy stood up and roared.

Clover covered his eyes. "That's it. I'm going to go shoot myself."

Louise cleared her throat and attempted to warn Frank of their close company. But, he was too busy tickling her side. "Frank," she said, acting as proper as she could, "behave yourself." She then put on a wide smile and pulled Uncle Frank across the road by his suspenders.

"Please tell me this is not what I think it is," Buddy pleaded.

"We're in love and plan to marry next month," Louise said matter-of-factly.

Uncle Frank gestured as if he was pulling a train whistle. "Gonna need a bachelor party, boys." He spoke with a louder than needed voice because of his advanced hearing loss.

"He's so cute," Louise said as she stepped back and admired him. "Well, we need to get my love bug to the doctor for a physical. We just want to make sure he's healthy."

Both Clover and Buddy had the look of disgust on their face. "Good grief," Clover began, "why don't you just fill my ears with jam and roll me around in an ant hill?"

Louise took Uncle Frank by the arm and led him back toward her house. "We'll see you later, boys," she said.

Buddy rose from his chair and walked to the edge of the porch. "Hey, if the doctor needs a stool and urine sample, just give him a pair of Uncle Frank's underwear," he yelled. Louise acted as if she did not hear the remark.

Both of the men sat back down and watched as Louise and Frank walked slowly away. "There they go, off like a herd of turtles." Clover remarked. He then looked over at Buddy.

"Looks like it's just you and me, again." Both men grunted and walked to their doors. A faint smile found its way on both their faces. Neither, of course, would ever admit how relieved they were.

Chapter 46

Angel was spending less time around the cottage in the afternoon since she and Jack began "taking walks" together. Each evening, after Jack finished his work for the day, he took Angel to Clawson's for dinner, after which they walked across the street to Taylor's Creek. The routine was consistent. Jack lifted Angel in his arms and walked her out until the water was chest deep. Then, together, they walked up and down the creek and watched people along Front Street. Angel was thrilled each time. And, even after four straight evenings of walking through the salty water, the novelty of it never dulled. The feeling of freedom that she had, as she walked, was simply indescribable. Only those who have lost such a necessary component of life, such as walking, can appreciate the euphoria of doing it again after so many years. She did have one worry, however. And, it was an important one. Would Jack eventually have ill feelings toward her, or her grandfather, as he had more time to think about the connection with Beverly? Would the fact that the professor's decision reduced her life to devastation and pain cause his feelings to fade? Angel knew, through her studies, that hurtful truths and feelings are sometimes controlled for a while, even years, but can fester at some point, ultimately causing an end to relationships. She knew this was a possibility. She also knew the equation of love and pain. *The greater you love something; the greater its potential to cause pain. They are directly proportional,* as she often said.

Without Angel around to talk to, the professor decided to go to Front Street and take a walk along the waterfront. On his way there, he took time to enjoy his surroundings, unlike his previous walks. There was a comfortable breeze, just cool enough to take away the sting of the summer heat and humidity. He noticed it was a quiet evening. There were no people walking dogs or sitting on their porch swings, waiting for a passerby to converse with. It was just a peaceful feeling. Why he never took the time to enjoy his surroundings, he did not know. When he finally reached Front Street and passed the corner pharmacy, he looked both ways for traffic. But, as he looked to the right, something caught his eye. At the meeting spot, under the oak tree, some two hundred yards away, he noticed there was one rocking chair, instead of two. Sitting in it appeared to be a woman. She was rocking gently, and appeared to be enjoying the sunset. The professor walked toward her to begin with, but increased his pace the clearer she became. "It can't be," he said to himself. At fifty yards away, he stopped and rubbed his eyes. Maybe it was his mind playing tricks on him, but the woman's golden hair and white button-down shirt reminded him so much of Sharon. His heart began pounding – the kind of pounding that happens after nearly having a car accident or when a rollercoaster pauses at the top of a drop. He ran for a few yards, then stopped, then walked and then jogged. And, the closer he got, the more the woman reminded him of Sharon. At ten feet away, he stopped completely and stood in complete disbelief.

"Sharon," he cried. "Sharon…" The woman did not answer. He took a few steps closer. "Sharon, is that you? Sharon…" He stepped closer. "Sharon…" His hands trembling, he reached out cautiously and touched the woman's shoulder. Her hand reached back and held his with a gentleness he could not misplace. When she finally turned to face him, he dropped to his knees and sobbed. "Dear God, Sharon. It can't be." He reached his hand up and touched her face. He expected his hand to go through her, given that she was a ghost. Instead, her skin was smooth and warm. Her face was full of color, her eyes as bright as when he first saw her. And, though she said nothing aloud, the kindness of her smile left no doubt that she was who she appeared to be. She motioned for the professor to stand and he did so. Then, after gazing into his eyes for what seemed an eternity, she wrapped her arms around him and pulled him close. The professor slowly lifted his arms and placed his hands on her back. He felt the beating of her heart, and the familiar fit, the one that felt so perfect, of her chest against his. And, what made it all the more real, was her smell - the faint, sweet smell of jasmine. It was how the professor remembered Sharon. It was the smell he loved from the first time he met her.

"How can this be, Sharon? You're dead. But, I can still feel you. I can still smell you." He continued holding her close and drank deeply from the warmth of her body. When the professor wept again, she placed her hands under his elbows and leaned back to face him.

"Michael," her voice was crisp and lovely, "I need you to know that I'm at peace; an incredible peace. It's wonderful where I am." She then pulled him close and again pressed her body against his. Resting her head against his chest, she whispered, "I love you, Michael. It's eternal. It never changes."

Chapter 47

The professor awoke from his sleep in a cold sweat. He looked around the dark room, but saw no signs of Sharon. He ripped the covers off his body and moved quickly to the living room and then the kitchen. But there was no sign of her.

"It can't be," he said. "I felt you. I felt your warmth; I felt your heart beat." He then dropped to his knees again and wept. "I felt you," he cried. "I felt you, Sharon." When he made it back to his feet, he searched the living room again, although he knew she would not be there. With unfathomable disappointment, he staggered back into the bedroom and sat down on the side of the bed. He placed his head into his hands and breathed slowly. "It can't be a dream," he tried to convince himself. But, he knew better. As he lifted his head, he noticed that Sharon's bible was missing from the nightstand. He was certain he placed it there. And, the more he thought, the more convinced he was that he had placed it there just before falling to sleep. "I know it was there," he mumbled. Then, as quickly as he could, he dressed himself, made his way through the front door, and headed to Front Street.

This time, when the professor arrived to the meeting spot, there were no apparitions of Sharon. Not that he expected any. And, just as in the dream, there was only one chair. It was perfect and pristine. And sitting in it was Sharon's bible. Inside was a single, folded sheet of paper. The professor sat in the chair, turned his back to allow the streetlight to illuminate the note and read:

Dear Professor,

There are two choices. You can choose to believe or not to believe. So, I ask you one last time - where's your faith?

T.L.

On the page where the note was placed, a verse was highlighted. The professor focused his eyes and made out the verse: Job 33:14-15.

Chapter 48

The professor sat in his leather chesterfield, placed his reading glasses on, and found the verse Timothy Lee had highlighted.

"For God does speak – now one way, now another – though man may not perceive it. In a dream, in a vision of the night, when deep sleep falls on men as they slumber in their beds." (Job 33:14-15)

"It simply can't be," the professor said. "She felt so real. She smelled so real." He closed his eyes and relived the dream. "It was different," he continued telling himself. "I can remember every detail. None of it is faded. It just felt…real."

"Grandpa, are you okay?" Angel's voice quickly brought the professor to the present.

"Yes, yes, I was just nodding."

Angel was still concerned. "It looked like you were talking to yourself. You said 'real'."

"Really, sweetie, I'm fine. Why are you up so early?"

Angel smiled and, yet, tears flowed down her face. "We need to talk."

It was a perfect afternoon to do as little as possible. But, for the professor, it was also an afternoon to feel the heaviness of a burdened heart. He sat on his front porch swing, sandwiched between the two unlikeliest of moral supporters.

"We're here for you, neighbor," Buddy said between an array of snorts and snots.

"That's right," Clover added, "you can count on us to get you through."

Next door, on Buddy's porch, a statically radio played a final song before the news came on.

At approximately 11:15 am, police arrested Timothy Lee Davis of Beaufort, after raiding his wooded camp off highway 101. Eyewitnesses spotted Mr. Davis' vehicle on Thursday evening, at around 9:00 pm, leaving the scene of a crime off Bakers Road, in the community of Harlowe. Three people were found shot to death, according to police. Mr. Davis is suspected of another slaying, approximately fifteen minutes later, of an elderly couple at the Front Street area of Beaufort. Police reports state that Timothy Lee Davis was questioned earlier this summer for a string of drug-related homicides. Thus far, authorities have not been able to conclusively place Mr. Davis at these locations. Further questioning will take place.

The professor pressed his fingertips against his forehead and closed his eyes. Buddy and Clover glanced over at each other.

"We tried to warn you about him, professor," Clover said. "But look, the good news is they've got him off the streets."

"I would have had him strung up in a tree way before now," Buddy snorted. "Just look at it as being one less thing to worry about." The professor kept his eyes shut and continued massaging his forehead. Buddy leaned forward and whispered, "You're safe now. Everything's going to be okay."

The professor sat up and shook his head. "He's innocent."

"He's what?" Buddy and Clover shouted at the same time.

"I'm sure of it. He was with me."

Chapter 49

"My name's Michael Valentine," the professor explained to the front desk clerk at the station, "and I was with Timothy Lee Davis on the night, or at least part of the night, he was accused of committing the homicides."

The woman pulled her headset off and looked disbelievingly at the professor. "You were with Timothy Lee on Thursday night? At the time of the crimes?" she clarified.

"Yes. I can attest that he was with me until at least nine o'clock. I remember he left at that time. He had somewhere to go. But, I can say for sure that he was with me from eight o'clock until nine o'clock."

"And how do you know Mr. Davis?" the lady asked sternly.

"I've met with him on a number of occasions over the two months. Beyond that, there's no connection."

The woman looked unimpressed by the professor's words. "You hold on a minute." She then disappeared down the hallway only to return a minute later. "Mr. Valentine, if you could just have a seat, somebody will be with you in about five minutes to take a statement."

The professor sat on the uncomfortable, lime-green couch for fifteen minutes when a well-dressed man finally appeared from the hallway. He greeted the professor with a handshake and then had him follow him down a long, labyrinth hallway, which led to a chamber. Once inside, the man pointed to a single chair that faced a large window covered by a curtain. When the professor sat down, the curtain opened and a man with long, unruly hair, tattooed arms and troubled eyes stared back at him.

"Mr. Valentine, can you identify this individual as being the man you were with on Thursday of this week?

The professor was baffled. "I said I was with Timothy Lee."

"This is Timothy Lee," the man replied.

The professor looked closely at the seemingly despondent man. "This isn't the man I was with."

Chapter 50

"Well, who the heck was he then?" Buddy exclaimed.

"I don't know," the professor answered. "He told me his name was Timothy Lee. He said he was a fisherman on Front Street. But, all I know is the man they showed me at the station was not the man I have been talking to."

"Are you sure he wasn't disguised?" Clover joined in.

"There's no way. The person I spent time with had kind eyes and a smooth face. I saw him as crazy only because of the stories I heard. The man at the station looked evil. He looked cold. He looked like the kind of person I would expect from the crimes he's committed."

"I don't understand." Buddy was bewildered.

"I only know what I saw. The man I knew was not Timothy Lee."

It was an hour later that Jack showed up for his usual afternoon walk with Angel. He was surprised when the professor answered the door. "Hey, Mr. Valentine, I'm just here to take

Angel to dinner." Jack immediately recognized the professor's look as being sympathetic. He knew the look well.

"She's not here, Jack," the professor said with a frown. "She left this for you."

Jack looked down at the note and then lifted his eyes to the professor. "Will she be back later?" He hoped the answer was not what his stomach told him it would be.

The professor held the noted closer to Jack's hands. "I'm sorry, Jack."

Jack walked back to the church slowly. He unfolded the note and began reading:

Dear Jack,

There are two kinds of people that teach and study the things I've shared with you - those that live them, and those that hide behind them. I guess you've figured out that I'm of the later group. I am being so selfish – so incredibly selfish – for doing what I've done. Please try to understand my reasons. This summer with you has been the most incredible months of my life. You've taught me so much more than I could ever teach you. Since the day I lost my ability to walk, it's all I've worked for and hoped to get back. The desire never left my mind. But, you – you've showed me that my life can have so much more if I could simply take my eyes off my legs and look at what is in front of me. You've showed me that I can love someone and, even more so, be loved by someone who doesn't care if I can walk or not. Jack, this time with you, I don't ever want to forget it. Everything that I've ever loved in my life has ended painfully. I know, Jack, that you do not think that my grandfather's mistreatment of your grandmother will ever change your feelings for me. But, the truth is, I know that at some point, it will. I do not want to ever look back at my time with you, and see anything less than what it was…perfect. Thank you for giving me such a wonderful time in my life. I will cherish it. I will cherish you.

If you ever make it to Chicago, look me up. Who knows, the law of attraction may bring us together again some day. But, if that never happens, please know that I love you, Jack. My words can never express how much.

Angel

When Jack arrived back to the church, he walked in, grabbed his blanket and pillow, locked the front doors and then drove away in his truck. A few minutes later, he arrived at Doug's house and knocked on his front door. When Doug answered, Jack collapsed in his arms and sobbed.

Chapter 51

The professor made the drive down winding roads, sur-rounded by marsh and water, until he arrived to the tiny fish-ing community of Mill Creek. The tide was high, allowing an occasional wave to lap across the highway. In the distance, he saw small wooden skiffs occupied by busy men throwing nets and squeezing the handles of tongs together in an effort to catch a batch of clams that was so much more precious to them than to those who would soon eat them. A clam to fish-ermen meant their family would have a roof over their heads and food for their children, for, at least, another day.

Just when he thought he was lost, the professor came upon a beautiful cathedral, tucked away in the wooded area across the road from the Newport River. A sign in the front read: The Finding Life Center. Pastor Chance Gordon.

Once inside he walked down a long, glass-covered hallway, lined with portraits of the men who founded and pastured at the church. When he found the office of Chance Gordon, he knocked lightly and then took a deep breath.

The door opened promptly. "Mike," Chance said enthu-siastically, "Come on in. I've been expecting you. Can I get you a cup of hot tea or coffee?"

"Hot tea would be nice, thank you," the professor answered. He then took a seat on the other side of Chance's desk. When Chance returned with the tea, he rolled his chair from behind his desk and placed it just near the professor's.

"Okay, may I say a prayer before we begin?" The professor affirmed with a nod of his head. Chance then held out his hands and placed them on top of the professor's. "Dear Heavenly Father, I ask that you would bless us on this glorious day and you would grant me with an open heart and a willing mind that I might be of your service and of some resolve for my brother, Mike. Thank you, Father, for your many blessings. Amen." Chance lifted his head and smiled at the professor. "Mike, how might I be of help?"

The professor, obviously uncomfortable, repositioned himself in his chair while convincing himself to ask the question. "Do you believe it's possible to see another person in a dream; but, it's more than a dream?"

Chance sat up in his chair. "You mean, does God allow us to see a loved one again after they have perished?"

"Yes," the professor answered simply.

"Well, to answer your question: Yes. I learned a lot about this from my grandfather. He also believed that God talked to us in dreams. In fact, there are many verses in the good book that attest to that."

"Such as Job 33?"

Chance grinned. "Such as Job 33, the fourteenth and fifteenth verses."

"So, you believe that I could see my wife in a dream and it not be just a dream?"

"I believe you can. But, there are some things that make a dream from God be more than just an ordinary dream."

"Such as?"

"Well, let me say this first. In that verse, it says: *For God does speak – now one way, now another.* Now, listen to this part: *though man may not perceive it.* Mike, God speaks to people all the time in dreams, but many people do not realize it. They push it off as just a dream. If only they would listen, they would hear the voice of God and be able to heed his wise counsel."

The professor thought back to the details of his dream. "So, how do you know it was real?"

Chance leaned forward and looked in the professor's eyes. "How do you know if you saw your wife? Correct?"

"Yes," the professor answered without elaboration.

"Many people do not believe that God speaks to us today through dreams. They believe dreams were used only under the Old Covenant. They believe God speaks to us today, in the New Covenant, through the Scriptures and His spirit. But, listen to what Peter tells us in Acts, chapter two, verse seventeen:" Chance grabbed a Bible off his desk and, very similarly to the man who called himself Timothy Lee, fanned through the pages until he found the right verse. "Peter says this: *In the last days, God says, I will pour out my Spirit on all people. Your sons and daughters will prophesy, your young men will see visions, your old men will dream dreams.*" Chance closed his Bible and looked back at the professor. "We live in the end times, Mike. Now, this verse doesn't mean only old men will see dreams. It's called Hebrew Parallelism. It paints a broader picture through the repetition of certain words. This means that old men, old women, as well as young men and young women can receive a dream from God. Joseph was only seventeen when God gave him a dream. Daniel and Solomon were young men when God gave them their dreams."

"But, how? How do you know?" the professor pushed.

"Well, let's talk about why He would give us dreams." Chance again grabbed his Bible and fanned through the pages. "Here," he ran his finger down the page, "in Ecclesiastes, chapter five and verse three. *A dream comes when there are many cares.*" Chance again closed his bible and smiled at the professor. "You see? In some cases, God will send a dream when we have worries, heartbreak...when we have cares. The question one may ask is why God sends one person a dream and not another. Unfortunately, that is not for us to understand."

"Can one know if the dream was sent or not?"

Chance took a moment to collect his thoughts. Gramps, my grandfather who started this church, taught me about two types of dreams we should really pay close attention to. One is a recurrent dream in which we dream the same, or similar, dream over days or weeks or longer. People who have recurring dreams should listen to them closely. The other kind of dream is a lucid or very clear and real feeling dream. Now, this kind of dream feels different from your usual, run-of-the-mill type dream. It is an amazingly clear dream. It doesn't become vague or foggy afterwards. You remember it vividly. This dream shows you details that you simply can't forget. It may even be so powerful that it wakes you from your sleep. It is a dream that you will still talk about twenty, thirty, forty years later. Sometimes the person in a dream may even talk to you. Those are really special dreams."

The professor again revisited his dream and recalled the very intense details of it. "Would you maybe *feel* the person in the dream, such as when you embrace them?"

"You may feel their chest beat, yes."

The professor's eyes lit up. "You could even smell them, yes?"

Chance stood and placed his hand on the professor's should. "Mike, you have been given a gift the rest of us could be envious of. You saw your wife again."

When they were finished, Chance walked the professor down the long, sunlit hallway. When they reached the front door, the professor shook Chance's hand and noticed his portrait on the wall. Beside it hung a picture of another young person, under which was a plaque that read: In loving memory of Charlie Robbins.

"Who is Charlie Robbins?"

"He was Dillon's father and my best friend. He's the friend I told you about who died of cancer. He saved my life when things had become very bleak. We built this church in his memory."

"So, this is a new church?"

"Well, not all of it." Chance pointed to a portrait of an older man that hung a little farther down the hallway. Under it read: "Gramps" Robbins. Founder. "That was mine and Charlie's grandfather. Everyone called him 'Gramps' around here."

The professor studied the picture. "He looks like a kind man."

"He was that, indeed."

The professor stared at the picture a moment longer. "Well, again, I thank you kindly for your time."

Chance shook his hand. "I hope you believe that God allowed you to see your wife again. It comes down to where you put your faith. You can have faith that you saw her. Or, you can have faith that you didn't."

"I'm not a believer," the professor admitted. Then, as he opened the front door to leave, he paused and looked back at

Chance. "What if you believers are wrong about there being a God?"

"Well, then, we've at least tried to live a noble life. And there's nothing wrong with that." The professor pursed his lips and hunched his shoulders. Then, as the door began to shut, Chance grabbed it. "Mike, what if *you're* wrong?" The professor paused and then walked away.

Chance said a quick prayer for the professor and then began his walk around the corner of the hallway that led to the sanctuary. Along those walls were another series of portraits. They chronicled Gramps' time in the church from its beginnings some fifty years earlier. For every few years that passed, there was a different picture of him. And, as the years made him younger, his name began to change. As Chance walked past the portrait of Gramps twenty years earlier, his name changed to T.L. Robbins. Then, when he reached the last picture on the wall, there was an early, vibrant looking picture of him. The picture showed a fairly young man, no older than forty-five. His curly brown hair was well trained -- not a single strand out of place. His face was smooth with freshly shaved cheeks that showcased eyes of piercing, deep green. His expression was alluring and, yet, tranquil. A persistent smile dominated the right side of the stranger's mouth and a faint sparkle made its home in the right eye, as well. Even his impeccably trimmed eyebrows were cared for with the utmost attention.

On a plaque beneath the portrait, it read:

Rev. Timothy Lee Robbins

Keep on loving each other as brothers.
Do not forget to entertain strangers,
for by so doing some people have entertained angels
without knowing it.

Hebrews 13:1-2

Epilogue

The ancient and wise have told it, those who listen to the nattering of dust and the cries of earth, that a cold wind will often move through us, shiver our heart and then carry away our sorrows, only to return them tempered and less robust. Five years later Jack's sorrow returned to him, though not as tempered as he would like.

His work had traveled him far, refurbishing churches across the country that time had moldered. He was working in the charming little town of Boulder, Colorado when he saw her again.

After finishing the last few details of the job, Jack stepped down from the scaffolding and patted the dust from his pants. A thin cloud of it drifted upward, causing him to fan it from his eyes. Up ahead, gazing through a store window was a woman that caught Jack's attention. He climbed back up the scaffolding to get a better view of her. When he was certain it was Angel, he walked up behind her and cleared his throat loudly.

"My ears won't stop vibrating," he said just loud enough for Angel to hear him, "It couldn't be that law of attraction."

"No," she exclaimed as she spun her chair around. "Jack!" They embraced briefly. "I can't believe it's you! What are you doing here?"

Jack felt numb and giddy at the same time. "I'm just finishing a job." He gestured to the church, "I'm still refurbishing churches. I travel a lot."

Angel looked over his shoulder to see the building. She then held his hand softly. "I knew you would do wonderful things." She then brushed her hand across his cheek. "Jack, I'm sorry for…"

"You don't need to apologize," he interjected.

"I wanted to call you, but I was just so ashamed."

Jack's voice was kind and gentle. "Really, it's okay. There's no need to explain."

Angel gazed into Jack's eyes as a sad smile pulled at her face. "Not a day goes by that I don't think back," she paused, "to our summer."

"Our summer," Jack agreed. "What became of your granddad?"

"Grandpa passed away about a year after I last saw you. Alzheimer's."

The answer made sense to Jack. "That's why he was forgetting so much."

"Yes," she answered.

"He was a good man. I never changed my mind about that."

Angel closed her eyes and nodded. "I was just so scared that you would."

"I would have never hurt you. And that's what hurt me the most: that you thought I would."

"I was weak, but just not willing to admit it."

"It's okay, Angel. I never stop smiling when I think back to that summer."

"Same here." Angel's eyes became moist and her lips quivered ever so slightly. "How crazy is it that we're here?"

"Well, if it really is that law of attraction, it sure took its time bringing you back to me."

Before Angel could reply, a toddler broke loose from a man's hand and ran straight for her. She leaped onto Angel's lap and wrapped her arms around her neck. "Mommy, Mommy," she cheered, "look what Daddy got me." She held up a doll.

Angel beamed up at Jack while the little girl prattled on about her new toy.

"She convinced me that you would approve," said a man who followed closely behind the child. He was of average height with dirty-blonde hair and dimples that appeared well used.

"Mark, this is Jack Dimmer. He's an old friend of mine from Beaufort." Angel looked back at Jack, "This is Mark, my husband."

The two men shook hands and exchanged smiles. "Beaufort, you don't say. What a beautiful little town. Only been there once, but I would love to get back there someday."

"It hasn't changed," Jack replied. He then looked back down at the little girl sitting contentedly in Angel's lap.

"And this is our daughter, Olivia," Angel answered before the question was asked.

Jack noticed Angel's features in the little girl. "She's beautiful," he admired. "Precious."

"You two just happened by each other?" Mark asked.

"All the way out here in Colorado," Jack answered.

Mark smiled and shook his head, "How's that for coincidence. This is our first time out here."

Jack gently tugged on his ear and grinned at Angel. "Quite a coincidence."

Mark looked at his watch and then glanced back at Angel.

"I know," she acknowledged, "we need to get moving if we want to make the train."

Jack also looked at his watch. "I need to get going, myself," he lied. "Angel, it was great running into you again. I'm happy for you." He then extended his hand to her husband. "Pleasure meeting you, Mark. If you're ever in Beaufort look me up."

"I'll be sure to."

Jack tipped his hat and turned to walk away.

"Jack," Angel stopped him. There was an awkward silence before she continued, "It was great seeing you again, too." She wanted to say more, but nothing came.

Jack smiled and walked away. A minute later, his phone rang. He checked the caller ID. "Hey sweetheart…I miss you, too…I'll be home tomorrow….Okay, I love you. Let me talk to Mommy. Daddy will see you when you wake up."

Whether the professor ever found belief in God, he did not openly reveal. Any time to do so was short. Alzheimer's disease is only fair in its equal ruin to all it encounters. It acted accordingly in the professor's brain, as it has in any other victim. Even so, the question of his faith was never a thought to the nurse-aid who was with him the final days of his life. Each night, as he lay like an infant, she sat by his side and joined him as he quietly hummed "Jesus Loves Me".

Printed in the United States
141528LV00001B/2/P

9 781438 965734